Two Yellow Dresses

The story line and the characters are totally fictional and any similarities to real life are purely coincidental.

t.a.wood author

cover illustrated by Katie Orchard

Two Yellow Dresses

Introduction

If you've ever been on a continental coach tour with an incompetent aggressive tour guide and with half the passengers being a bunch of obnoxious individuals, you'll relate to this story. The main characters are Jill and Jenny, very attractive teenagers, find themselves victimised by the tour guide from the moment they meet, and eventually make a bold decision but still cannot escape her venomous intentions.

~~~~~Two Yellow Dresses~~~~~

Day one Sunday

For the past six months Jenny and Jill both teenage student nurses have planned and constantly talked about their first continental holiday, and at long last the day has arrived. Excited but nervous they boarded the aeroplane for their first ever flight and settled into their seats as the plane roared on the runway waiting for a take off slot. The noise from the Boeing 737's engines intensified as the aeroplane began to judder and pick up speed, Jenny made a note in her diary.... '8.12am September 6th. 2015 took off from Gatwick'.

From the very first moment they stepped from the plane at Salzburg airport the two girls sensed a strong feeling of animosity towards them emanating from a vision in a flame red uniform waiting to greet the party of new arrivals.

The forty strong group gathered around this imposing mass of red womanhood who promptly and abruptly introduced herself as 'Rose your tour guide' and as quickly as she had completed a head count, ushered the party out to a waiting luxury coach with it's red demon emblems emblazoned along the sides and across the front and rear, laid over the vivid yellow painted body of the smart vehicle.

With everybody now seated aboard the bus and for those who weren't listening the first time she repeated at full volume with the aid of a microphone. "I'm Rose your tour guide for the next sixteen days, and as long as you do what I say we'll all get along very well and you'll all have a wonderful time". "Yes mien Fuhrer". Someone at the back of the coach with a black country accent retorted, although not with the intention of it coming out as loud as it did, creating laughter from those brave enough to be identified.

"We're off now to check in to our first hotel in the centre of Salzburg and this afternoon the bus will take you on a site seeing tour of the city. That is as soon as those two selfish females decide to join us". Rose blasted loud enough for the two attractive teenagers to hear as they raced across the tarmac road surface and breathlessly scrambled on to the coach, leaving their luggage on the paving for the driver to stow away in the hold compartment.

"Your driver is Giovanni, he speaks good English and he'll be safely driving you throughout your tour of the beautiful Austria, Switzerland and Italian lakes and mountains, finishing in Naples from where you fly back to Britain. That is as soon as he's put these two selfish girls bags away". She repeatedly scolded the girls who had now occupied the remaining empty pew and sitting silently, petrified by this vindictive woman, and too afraid to speak out in their defence, that one of their luggage bags and not come through and that Rose knew of this.

"There aren't any porters at this hotel so as soon as you've collected your luggage go and book in and be back here on the pavement outside the hotel in thirty minutes". The guide woman screeched unceremoniously.

The rumblings of immediate dissatisfaction rippled through the bus as they watched Rose in the red uniform looking idly on as Giovanni struggled single handed unloading the various shapes and sizes of suitcases and holdalls and stacking them in the hotel reception area.

"My God she's a bundle of fun, she must have been taught the hospitality industry when she was in the Hitler Youth Movement". A tall elderly grey haired male passenger remarked. "She doesn't seem to like you two kids". He added in a Geordie accent as he wandered past the nineteen year old teenagers as they sat waiting for a gap in order to stand and join the compact queue shuffling along in the aisle to get off the bus.   .

"Two hours gives you plenty of time to find some lunch. The Mirramarble gardens are a few minutes walk, that's were Maria sang and danced with the Von Trapp kids on the steps. Back here at three o'clock sharp, we are then going to see the castle, so no one be late". The woman in red demanded.

"I think she means the Mirabell gardens". Another member of the group remarked. "She hasn't got a clue, you'd think she'd get her facts rights, she's supposed to be a rep". The fellow from the black country murmured quietly.

"This is my first tour with this company but I do know my way around Salzburg. So if any of you want to come along with me". Rose invited in her accustomed dictatorial loud shouty voice to which half a dozen party members responded and duly followed in her footsteps, leaving the 'more sensible' majority of the group to disperse as couples or with newly formed friends.

"What is it with this evil woman, all we did was to tell her we wasn't going to the castle and we'd make our own way back to the hotel and she went berserk". Jill at five feet eight inches tall, the shorter of the two girls cursed. "The less time we're in her company the better, the old sod". Jenny replied. "Some holiday this is going to be". She added as they wandered down one of the pretty narrow streets admiring all the elaborate hanging signs and looking for somewhere to eat.

The engine of the luxury continental touring bus purred gently in the mid afternoon sunshine oblivious to the atmosphere already festering within. The tanned smart male driver in a pristine white open neck shirt, adorned with the company badge depicting a demon sewn on to the breast pocket, sat relaxing with both arms resting across the steering wheel.

The coach full of mostly annoyed

passengers all fastened in their seats, except for a couple of oversize irate lady travellers standing in the aisle seething, all urgently awaiting the return of the two teenage girls.

Jill and Jenny, both very attractive tall slim teenagers excitedly experiencing their first continental holiday, completely unaware of the fury on board the coach, strolled aimlessly enjoying the sunshine and the surroundings and the attention of a couple of handsome local youths.

"Sorry folks, that's it, there isn't enough time left to visit the castle now. I suggest the coach stays here for another hour while you have a wander round or get yourselves a coffee or go back in the gardens". Rose suggested to a few groans and murmurings of disappointment. "Well we all know who to blame". Rose added vindictively.

The air could be cut with a knife as Jill and Jenny, looking extremely elegant in their choice of evening wear, Jenny in a slim fitted emerald green dress and Jill's choice being a smoke grey dress and a matching lightweight jacket. They sensed a multitude of pairs of eyes all staring furiously in their direction, the women folk mainly in envy as the girls stood in the open doorway to the dining room anxiously scanning the tables and unable to see any empty seats.

Both girls strikingly attractive, Jenny with her jet black glossy hair resting on her shoulders and Jill the complete contrast with long honey blonde hair floating half way down her back.

Hesitantly they ventured into the room, completely puzzled at some of the other guests reaction to their presence, until a measly looking fellow with his napkin tucked into his shirt collar muttered out loud. "Here they are, these are the ones who caused us to miss going to the castle". "They can't even be on time to come down to dinner". His wife, another oversize woman snarled as though she'd just eaten a dish of wasps for her starter.

"Shut up you stupid woman, you're just jealous that you can't and never did look like that". The familiar Brummie voice called out, to an instant reprimand from his wife.

"Hold on a minute". Jenny nervously shouted. "We told Rose that we wasn't going to the castle and we wouldn't come back to the coach and that we intended to make our own way back to the hotel". "Oh no you didn't, you never said any such thing". The trade mark voice of Rose boomed for the whole hotel to hear as she entered the room and made her way to a singles table in the corner of the room.

"You liar". Jenny screamed, and realising the the ensuing slanging match would only increase the pressure on the girls to leave the room, an elderly lady and her companion called them across to their table.

"This is your table my dears, there was two places set here when we came in, but now we know why they were removed. Nasty woman !" The younger of the two ladies said, the latter words spoken in a whisper as she beckoned the waiter to return the chairs and reset the places.

"Honestly, we told her that we would make our own way back to the hotel". Jill reiterated, desperately trying not to allow any tears. "Perhaps she misunderstood you". "No, that's impossible, anyway it's no way for anyone to treat their guests, she should never be in this job". Jenny the stronger willed of the two girls said out loud enough with the deliberate intention of it reaching the ears in the far corner of the room.

"Anyway I'm Edith and this is my older sister Georgina, she's the quiet one". "I'm Jill and she's my best pal Jenny. We've known each other since we were four, we've been best friends since our very first day at school". Jill said passionately as the girls and the sister's arms entwined in an introductory shaking of hands. "I wonder what delightful little surprises she's got in store for us tomorrow". Jenny joked sarcastically as they wished the elderly ladies a pleasant evening stroll.

~~~~~~~~~~~~~~~~~

The bright early morning beckoned the tourists to the luxury yellow and red coach, clean and shining brilliantly in the sunshine ready for another day of sightseeing. Like obedient lemmings they trailed one after the other and climbed the two small steps and took their new seating positions according to the strict daily rota enforced by the red uniformed courier. Today the front and most coveted seats were reserved and deserted, awaiting for the arrival of the teenage girls. The driver took advantage of the long delay to study his new route as the noisy throng grew more impatient in the heat of the stationary vehicle, desperately in need of it's air conditioning to be fully functioning.

The call to go without them came loud and clear from a couple of the oversize ladies who had earlier pronounced their allegiance to the red uniform.

Rose the tour guide is a stern arrogant giant of a woman, totally out of her depth for the job she commanded. A picture to behold in her bright red pleated skirt, which only emphasizes her size even more, with identical colour blazer and the red face to complete the set.

In a rage she scurried back into the hotel and returned dragging Jenny, the slightly taller of the two girls by the sleeve of her sweater, as a head mistress would a naughty school child, until it became detached from her arm, making the sleeve some three inches longer. Jill tagged along laughing hysterically at the expression of surprise on her friend's face.

The girls took up their front row seats, both looking fresh in their individual coloured flared skirts and plain white sweaters, albeit that Jenny now appeared to possess one arm longer than the other, with both Jill and Jenny sporting a stylish straw sun hat.

"Now we've been delayed yet again". The 'Red Demon', as the girls and most of the other guests had already Christened her, adopting the company logo as a suitable comparison, shouted sarcastically while perching herself on the windscreen bulkhead, completely obliterating any advantage of occupying the front seats. Then with a microphone in her left hand, bellowed to the driver his instruction to set off, probably destroying his right ear drum in the process as he sat just a couple of feet away. And to attempt to embarrass the girls even more, shouted again using her microphone, that had it not been a day for travelling to a new destination and a new hotel the coach would have left without them.

Giovanni, the coach driver, a relaxed carefree handsome sun tanned Italian casually steered the long vehicle away from the hotel and at the same time gave the girls a secret smile and a cheeky wink as the coach began to travel at speed along the lake side.

After a couple of kilometres the lake disappeared and the coach began a steep ascent into the mountains. The days commentary began with a loud tap on the end of the microphone followed by some useless information about cow bells and mountain meadows as RD, the abbreviated version now accepted and being openly used, told the uninterested passengers except for a select few who are intent on being her support group and listen to her every word.

After a hour and a half the coach reached it's highest point and the driver skilfully reversed the bus between a pair of yellow parallel lines.

"Wait.....wait". Demanded RD as her passengers began to leave the coach and head for the restaurant and the scenic view point. "The bus leaves in exactly one hour, so be here by two o'clock or we leave without you". RD screeched as if she was an army sergeant drilling a new platoon of squaddies on the parade square, causing several male passing tourists alighting from an adjacent coach to jump to attention with a salute and raised laughter.

"One of these days someone will give her a gentle shove over a cliff". Jill joked as they queued in the self service section of the restaurant with their respective trays of food. "It might be sooner than you think". Jenny the slightly taller slim nineteen year old girl with jet black hair, and one sleeve noticeably longer than the other, replied with a laugh.

The spectacular view from the rear of the restaurant, with it's deep ravine to the glacier the size of the largest lake spread out below, protected only by a one metre high galvanised steel barrier, with the snow capped awe inspiring mountain peaks all around encompassing the perfect photo shot.

"I heard you two in the queue plotting to get rid of the red demon. I'll tell you what, you call her over and we'll draw straws and the lucky winner gives her a push". A sixty something fellow passenger joked as he sidled up to the girls and leaned on the barrier.

"Don't take any notice of the old sod, we're supposed to be on holiday, not a bloody army exersize". He added. "I'm Joe, my missis is Mave. Not everybody on the coach is bothered that your time keeping is a bit off, you two girls are the only breath of fresh air on this bus, so just enjoy yourselves and bugger that woman". He continued in his strong black country accent. "Anyway we'd better be getting back to the coach or we might get the cane or detention".

RD was again perched on the windscreen bulkhead with her feet resting on the chrome grab rail showing Giovanni a yellow water tight bag she'd just purchased from the gift shop. When the girls returned and attempted to enter the bus, RD deliberately let her foot slide along the rail and kick Jill's hand. "Oh...sorry". She uttered sarcastically and repeated the manoeuvre on Jenny. "Ignorant sod". Jenny murmured under her breath.

"Now that you've all got to know each other...you can call me Rose....Rose Devlin.

That's my name on the itinerary sheet. I notice some of you have already decided to abbreviate it to RD, but I would prefer Rose". The vision of this woman in the bright red uniform being a rose is akin to calling a ferocious wild tiger Tiddles.

"Right are we all present ? Anyone not here...tough !" The friendly courier announced, without even a glance through the coach to check for any empty seats. The coach door automatically closed and the party settled down for a further two hour drive through the Austrian scenery and on to Innsbruck for a two night stay.

The tittering and laughter created by the coincidence of the RD reference to her demon comparison went totally unnoticed by Rose as she constantly bombarded her passenger's ears with more and more unwanted, useless and to the more seasoned travelling guests, utter incorrect rubbish. Although to a small contingency of half a dozen passengers, her word was Gospel. These three couples clung to her like school class creeps and dissociated themselves from the majority of the party.

That evening the girls again found that RD had isolated them from the rest of the group for dinner and insisted that unfortunately because of the limited size of the dining room, that their table was in a side room at the rear of the hotel just off the main room

Jenny the more forceful of the two girls refused to sit in the dingy back room and holding Jill by the hand marched back into the main dining room and promptly sat in the two adjacent vacant chairs. "What's wrong with you ? These seats are obviously for me and Jill". Jenny screamed as RD stood seething with noticeable rage. "Good on yer girl". Joe their new found black country friend voiced his solitary support. "Why do you keep picking on me an Jill ? We've paid for a holiday, not to be hassled every minute of the day by a useless jumped up rep". Jenny blasted with Jill looking on. Her mouth wide open in disbelief, not quite recognising her friend's sudden transformation from her normal calm persona.

With her heart pounding in her chest like a steam hammer, Jenny was surprised as she watched RD, all dressed up for the evening in a lime green trouser suit, topped off with a fuming red flushed face, storm from the room without a word of retaliation. "Now that Kermit's buggered off we can all enjoy our meal". Joe added again defiantly in his distinctive accent.

"Thank God we've got the whole day to ourselves tomorrow, perhaps she's got the message and she'll leave us alone". Jill said turning to Georgina sitting by her side. "By the look of her when she stormed out, at the moment dear, I think your friend may have just made things a whole lot worse. At least you got rid of her for the rest of the evening. I'm Georgina, this is my sister Edith, we're from Southampton".

"Yes we know, we sat with you last night, don't you remember ?" Jenny asked politely realising an awkward moment. "You'll have to excuse my sister, unfortunately she has early signs of dementia. Her memory isn't what it used to be". Edith whispered. "Most days she's perfectly alright and you wouldn't even notice". She added. "We did think it was something like that, we're used to it, we're both nurses, we work in the same hospital, so don't worry we understand". Jenny replied sympathetically.

"You're very brave to bring her on holiday, but why not, we get to see so many poor devils just abandoned in homes. Everybody needs some company, and except for her memory we wouldn't have realised she had the illness". Jenny responded.

"You two girls are very kind, we do get problems occasionally. You seem very young to be nurses, how old are you ?" Edith enquired respectfully. "I must admit I exaggerated a little bit, we're only trainee nurses yet, but we do get thrown in the deep end quite often. We're both nineteen, in fact we were both born on the same day, so we adopted each other as twins". Jenny explained slightly embarrassed by her initial omission. "The odd coincidence is that I really am a twin. I have a twin sister living in America who I haven't seen, since we were three years old, and I can't even remember her. I also have a sixteen year old half brother. All I've seen are photographs that my sister has sent me over the last few years that we've been constantly in touch.

The main reason we chose this holiday is that this was the only tour I could find that had an excursion to Venice on the same day that my sister and my brother would be there. They're on a world cruise with my mum and her second husband. I've arranged to meet up with them in Saint Marks Square". Jenny said breathlessly and paused to draw an intake of air.

"How did you come to be parted from your twin sister at three years of age ? If you don't mind me asking". Edith enquired respectfully. "My parents split up and they agreed to have a child each, well apparently dad had to agree, he didn't want us to be parted. Mum insisted she only wanted one of us, so dad had no choice other than to have just me. The intention was that they kept in touch and us twins would still see each other regularly, but within a couple of months she went off with her new man to live in America. My sister and I have been in touch for the past few years, but I promised my dad that I'd never contact my mum. Not that I could have ever afforded to go to America and I know from my sister that her husband wouldn't allow her to contact me either". Jenny replied at length. "But at last I'm going to meet my twin sister again". She added excitedly. "If you don't mind me saying that's such a sad story and I think it was a terrible thing to do to separate you two sisters at three years old, especially twin sisters". Edith responded quite annoyed.

"I agree, it nearly killed our dad, I don't

think he's ever got over mum leaving let alone splitting us up". Jenny replied.

"What are you having for your main course tonight Georgina ?" Edith asked of her sister in order to involve her in the conversation. "I think my baby sister's joking. I'll have what comes, and so will you and everybody else, it's a set meal. We don't get a choice". Georgina teased.

~~~~~~~~~~~~~~~~~

Day three Tuesday

At this stage of any normal group holiday the guests have usually aligned themselves with other like minded travellers and formed various degrees of friendships, while at the same time deliberately avoiding the ones not liked. As has almost, but not quite happened with this tour of the lakes and mountains of Austria, Switzerland and Italy, which commenced with a flight to Salzburg and concludes with a return flight to the UK from Naples. On this particular trip less than half of the passengers can be classed as decent ordinary folk, mainly pleasant easy to get along with people who would probably prefer to keep themselves to them self. But not to mince words, the rest of this bunch are plainly nasty, arrogant and obnoxious a group of people you could ever not want to meet anywhere, let alone in the confines of a coach for sixteen days.

Joe and Mavis from Smethwick in the West Midlands together with Edith and Georgina and also John an ex Royal Marine from Gateshead and his lady companion Lucy have befriended Jill and Jenny, the two attractive nineteen year old girls after disagreeing with the consistent bullying of the girls from RD the courier, and the nasty majority of the party. Mostly emanating through envy from the not so attractive women of the group. The worst culprit for this level of abuse being RD herself, for some unknown reason she has entered into a vendetta with the girls from the moment she first saw them.

Joe and his wife Mavis both at five feet nine inches tall, being ideally suited in height and personalities and not an ounce of fat between them make the perfect couple. Both now reduced to greying hair, but still plenty of it. Joe always freshly clean shaven and smelling of a pleasant quality soap, Mavis with her nineteen fifties style perm and make up to suggest she may once have been on the stage. Albeit they appear a bit rough around the edges and a little bit outspoken they make the ideal couple for Jill and Jenny to associate with.

RD being an abbreviation for 'red demon' which just coincidently happens to be her real initials and also the name of the company and it's logo. Up to yet RD has not realised her not very flattering comparison to the company demon logo, or if she is aware she is too embarrassed to acknowledge it. The red prefix very well suited to the flaming colour of her extra large uniform and in most circumstances, her face.

The party have already, even amongst the nasty element, split between the majority who have formed a dislike her and the half a dozen who treat her like the pied piper.

"You have the whole day free here in Innsbruck. I'm off on a cable car to Mount Igls". RD shouted across the dining room floor to her group enjoying their croissants and jams.

"She's got that wrong as well, Igls is the village, the mountain is the Patscherkofel". A bright spark 'know all' named Douglas, already earned the cruel label by a few of the menfolk as Dug the bug.

Douglas, a shortish man standing no more than five feet two inches high and some sixty odd years old, as yet not seen without his maroon club blazer, grey flannels and cream coloured cravat, and always with a map and a note pad on his lap. When seen standing along side his six feet tall wife they cut the oddest of couples. Heather his wife, slim and extremely attractive and elegant, Douglas, short, plump and not to put to finer point on it, bloody ugly. His only notable asset, being one of the most vitriol of RD's enemy.

The usual three couples who by now tended to gather together for meals and outings began to leave the breakfast table. The three women stayed seated for a while and slyly stuffed the spare ham rolls into their day bags before sheepishly following the men.

"Anyone coming with me, meet me in the hotel lobby in a quarter of an hour". RD again shouted across the room. "Oh good a whole day without her, we'll stay in Innsbruck". Jill said gleefully. "I think we're going to climb to the top of the ski jump first". Jenny informed Joe and Mavis, their table companions this morning. "The Bergisel ski jump". A squeaky informative voice called out. "Oh God that Duggie bloke's going to get on my nerves with his soddin' note book". Mavis responded.

"We'll come along with you two girls, if you don't mind". Joe suggested. "No you won't you old flirt, Jill and Jenny have their own plans. You're taking me round the town and the shops and then for a nice lunch at an outdoor cafe". Mavis said with a sneaky smile to the teenagers.

"You'd better give our Betty a ring, see how she's getting on with Yabuga before we go anywhere". Mavis instructed her husband, "He's our dog". She added for the benefit of Jill and Jenny, already in fits of laughter.

With great difficulty Jill composed herself and asked. "What did you say his name was ?" "Yabuga, he got Christened that because Joe kept being told off for swearing at him when he wouldn't come back. He tells people it's Russian". Mavis replied, also laughing uncontrollably. "It's not his real name is it ?" Jenny asked. "Yes it is, it's on his pet insurance and with the vets. He was a rescue dog so it's also registered with the kennels". Mavis added seriously between the hysterical giggling.

Jenny and Jill left the breakfast table and walked through to the lift in the reception area with tears streaming down their faces to the amusement of the few remaining guests. Mavis and Joe followed a few moments later, Joe rigidly maintaining a stern face, pretending not to be amused while his wife Mavis was almost bent double with infectious laughter.

With the knowledge of RD being somewhere half way up a mountain. The teenage girls relaxed in the warm morning sunshine while still bursting into spontaneous laughter at the thought of Joe calling his dog. They strolled to the entrance to the Olympic ski jump and stared up to it's highest point.
  "Rose reckons she can ski, I'd give anything to see her come hurtling down that slope on her backside and flying straight into the cemetery. Talk about Eddie the Eagle, she could be Rosie the Rocket. If she comes here I'd willingly give her a little starter push".Jenny laughed.
  "It looks a bit different to the way dad described it. He reckoned him and mum climbed the steps all the way to the top. He never mentioned anything about a cable car or a restaurant". Jill muttered. "Well I supposed it's changed over the years, you're talking about twenty five years ago". Jenny replied. "Anyway let's go in, how much is it ?"
  After a brief cable car journey and the internal lift Jill and Jenny spent the next hour pleasantly drinking coffee and admiring the panoramic view of the surrounding mountains, resplendently capped with snow and enhanced by a clear blue cloudless sky.
  "Did you notice how this morning RD seemed to be very friendly with everyone else except us ?" Jill asked. "Yes. I think someone

has phoned in and complained about her. Perhaps she'll get round to liking us if we phone in and complain, or better still, let's do a bit of creeping round her like her little group of pets". Jenny quipped with a sarcastic snigger "I doubt it, anyway let's go and find somewhere cheaper to have lunch". She added.

"We'll soon know if we've been chosen as her favourite girl couple, she's coming to this cafe with her followers". Jill whispered as RD and two couples sat beneath the large multi coloured sun umbrella at an adjacent table.

"Oh...hello you two, we didn't see you there". One of the husbands chirped politely, taking Jill and Jenny completely by surprise. "We didn't think you'd be back so soon, have you had a good morning ?" Jill asked in order to strike up a friendly conversation. "Our wives didn't want to do the cable car, so we just spent an hour in the village". He answered as he was joined by his wife shuffling her chair to face the girls to the annoyance of RD.

"Are you two eating with us ?" RD shouted abruptly. "That answers that, we're definitely not on her Facebook page. I think it's you two she means". Jenny murmured.

"You're sitting with us tonight". Joe said as Jill and Jenny searched for a couple of empty chairs. "Have you had a good day ?" Mavis asked. "Yes we had a lovely day, we went up to the restaurant at the top of the ski jump this morning". Jill replied. "We went there in the afternoon, fantastic place, how do they go down that slope and take off into mid air ? So steep, it frightened me just looking at it". Mavis added.

"Our lunch was slightly spoilt. We sat outside to eat and who do you think came and sat at the next table ?" Jenny moaned. "Not RD ?" "Yes" "I was hoping she was going to get lost on that bloody mountain". Joe chuntered. "They never did the cable car. The one couple in the group actually turned their chairs to face me and Jenny until she ordered them back in line". Jill chirped. "Serves them right, poor sods". Joe quipped.

"It's soup tonight for the starter...it's always soddin' soup. I just hope it's one I like". Joe said as a young pretty Austrian girl in traditional dress approached the table balancing four dishes, one in each hand and the others on her inner forearms. "I still don't know what it is, but at least it's hot". Joe stated as he tasted the liquid.

"How was you dog ?" Jenny asked causing Mavis to spill a spoonful of soup into the napkin on her lap as she erupted into laughter. "Don't ask about the dog, it's his soddin' pigeons I really worry about. He only rang up the Red Demon Tour Company to see if they would let him bring a basket of his best racing pigeons. He offered to pay for their flight". Mavis said and immediately burst into laughter again as she uttered the word 'flight'. "He told them he'd loose them up as soon as the plane lands in Salzburg, so he wouldn't be taking them on the coach". Mavis added and nearly choked on a bread roll.

"Did they say no ?" Jenny asked exploding into hilarious laughter which became infectious throughout the occupants of the adjacent tables as well as theirs. "I wouldn't mind but he really thought they were being unreasonable, daft sod". Mavis said as she totally lost control and covered her face with her soup stained napkin to hide the tears of laughter streaming down her face. Joe remained silent and just winked at the girls.

Joe carried on eating his evening meal unperturbed by the laughter and mockery emanating from his wife and the teenagers, while at the same time bubbling beneath the surface until he couldn't contain himself any longer and also burst into laughter.

"Are you going to the Tyrolean evening in the hotel tonight ?" Joe asked. "Lots of leather and backside slapping". He added with a snigger. "I suppose so, do you want to stop in Jill ?" Jenny asked her friend. "Might as well we've done enough walking for one day". Jill replied. "You girls should enjoy it, lots of brawny Austrian lads in shorts and braces. Mind you once you've seen one Tyrolean evening you've seen the lot. You'll probably get another one tomorrow night. Me and Mave must have seen at least a dozen". Joe concluded.

"We're off to Switzerland in the morning, have you two ever been to Lucerne ?" Joe asked Jill and Jenny. "No neither of us has ever been abroad before, this is the first time we've even had a holiday out of England". Jill replied. "We've never even been to Wales or Scotland either". Jenny interrupted with a giggle.

"You'll enjoy Lucerne, we had a fantastic hotel right on the lake a couple of years ago when we did a great train holiday". Joe informed his captive audience, as they waited patiently to be told the choice of sweets.

~~~~~~~~~~~~~~~~~

Day four Wednesday

The sound of Tyrolean music played over the audio system as the coach cruised effortlessly through the Austrian landscape. The rich or ripe as the case maybe passengers for once silently enjoying the peaceful atmosphere, with RD seemingly having received an injection of friendliness serum, at last performing as a holiday courier should, sat on her perch next to the driver.

Sitting mid way along the bus Jenny had nodded off to sleep in the window seat with her head cushion off the glass pane by her straw sun hat. Jill's mind and imagination wandered as she cast her eyes around the coach wondering what sort of lives her fellow passengers lived.

There was Joe and Mavis sitting directly opposite across the aisle in complete silence, most unusual for Joe to miss a chance to chat up the girls. Perhaps that's why Mavis made him sit in the window seat. A nice fun loving couple in their mid sixties, a bit rough and ready, but a good honest to goodness couple with strong black country accents.

Jill attempted to stifle her giggles as she began to rekindle her thoughts about the story of their dog and Joe's pigeons and wonder if her and Jenny were just having their legs pulled as Mavis turned and smiled and mouthed silently. "Are you alright Jill". Jill nodded.

Jill stared with admiration at the elegant profile of Douglas's wife Heather, sat on the same side as Mavis and Joe, but a couple of pews further towards the front. As per usual Duggie occupied the window seat, and most certainly to have a map of the current route on his lap and a biro between his teeth. 'What on earth does she see in him, how did they ever meet'. Jill pondered to herself.

Sitting in front of Heather, John was creating a bit of interest. A tall upright six foot something rugged man in his eighties, but still retaining his good looks with a full head of hair, now a shade of silvery grey, stood in the aisle to retrieve a magazine from the overhead compartment. An ex army marine and retired steel erector from Tyneside, a widower travelling with an attractive well dressed lady companion some twenty years his junior.

At the very front of the coach Jill watched the back of RD's mousey brown head bobbing from side to side as she tried in vain to engage Giovanni in conversation. This was short lived as she switched her pose to face a couple in the coveted front pew. 'Glad we're not sitting there, mind you she is being pleasant at the moment'. Jill thought with her imagination loitering somewhere in cloud cuckoo land.

'What's this ?'. Jill wondered as the robust figure in the red uniform stood and turned to face down the bus.

Jenny and probably most of the rest of the passengers jumped out of their skins when RD bellowed throughout the length of the vehicle. "In about fifteen minutes we will arrive in Feldkirch. We'll stop for a couple of hours. It's a lovely medieval town and you'll have plenty of time to look around and find some lunch. It's now twenty past twelve, so we'll all, that's everybody, be back at the coach at three o'clock".

"She might be being friendly and doing her job properly at the moment but by the sound of that announcement it didn't include me and you". Jenny snapped.

"Three o'clock". RD screeched a reminder across the coach park as the last of her passengers disappeared into an alleyway and into the pretty medieval town centre to be greeted by a fantastic party atmosphere.

"Of course Duggie the Bug new all about it and was only too eager to share his knowledge with anyone in earshot. "It's the region's wine fest, they're celebrating the wine harvest". He spouted to the one and only couple who'd been polite enough to stop and listen.

A continuous line of arches leading into a covered walkway flanked the whole length of both sides of the street, with several of the shops within the corridors providing wine to the hoards of people, mostly local folk. The middle of the street was completely taken over by a continuous line of trestle tables and seating for the happy crowd of drinkers.

Within minutes Jill and Jenny were being rigorously involved in handshaking and partially forced to join a very friendly local farming family at one of the tables. The girls sat mesmerised as two young lads began chatting away in German. "Sorry we don't understand, we're English". Jenny said slowly and deliberately with the emphasis on the word 'English'. "Oh....you're from England....Bobby Charlton...Stanley Matthews...Big Ben". The tall blonde Austrian lad said, keen to show off his knowledge of England. "I can speak England he added, my brother he can not". He added with great pleasure to have someone to practice on. Jill hesitated whether to correct him to say English but decided to be diplomatic and remain silent.

He then, over a period of the next five minutes carefully explained to the girls that they have to go to any one of the shop windows in the covered corridors that are serving wine. "You have to buy your first glass of wine, bring your drink back and sit with us and when your glass is empty you go back to the window and it will be filled again, you do not have to pay again, it is free. You keep the glass as a souvenir". He proudly said in his best English. Throughout the language lesson his brother, the more handsome of the two, sat secretly smiling and flirting with Jenny and immediately jumped to his feet, beating his younger blonde haired brother to escort the girls to fetch their drinks.

After the second successive refill of white wine in their 1/4 litre commemorative glasses the girls began to get a touch of 'the giggles'.

"I think we ought to look for some lunch while we're still capable". Jenny stuttered slightly intoxicated. "Bye fellas". Jill chirped, and as they stood to leave the table the whole family, seven males of various ages and three middle aged ladies all kissed the girls in turn on both cheeks.

"Well that was different". Jenny laughed as she wobbled into Jill causing them both to lean against an arch pillar for support.

"Thank goodness I've bumped into you girls, can you help me ?" A distraught Edith screamed shakily as Jill and Jenny sat in the shade of an archway enjoying a light salad lunch. "Georgie's gone missing. I only left her for a minute to fetch some drinks and when I got back to the table she'd gone". Edith cried out, now quite panic stricken. "I shouldn't have left her, she was having one of her bad spells. Stupid....stupid me". She cursed herself.

"She can't be far away, split up, we'll find her. Meet back at the coach". Jill suggested encouragingly as Edith and Jenny set off in separate directions while Jenny beckoned the elderly lady waitress.

Edith and Jenny stood leaning against the side of the coach for support in the hot afternoon sunshine talking to Giovanni and waiting hopefully to see Jill come through the alleyway holding Georgina by the hand. Edith began sobbing hysterically when Jill came in to view alone.

With nearly everyone else sat stifling in the stationary bus, RD blurted out in her uncompromising voice. "We can't wait much longer". "You can't leave !" Jenny screamed. "I'm in charge of this coach, and if I say we're leaving.....we're leaving". RD screamed back.

"I'm in charge of this bus...you are in charge of your guests......so look after them". Giovanni the driver scolded angrily forcing RD to turn and wander away from the coach to avoid any further embarrassment.

Edith and the girls together with Giovanni immediately set off back into the busy throng of the partying wine drinking local population followed by the majority of RD's passengers as they poured from the coach.

After three parts of an hour some of the guests had dribbled back and were waiting anxiously in groups by the coach being lectured to by RD.

"Stupid woman, fancy bringing someone on holiday with dementia, especially a coach tour". Muttered a short arrogant older woman, one of the nasty section, whom Joe had previously encountered when she mouthed off at Jill and Jenny. and given her the name of Missis Gobby. "Doesn't her sister know that dementia is a terminal illness ? She should be in a home". She snarled unsympathetically and annoyed at being delayed.

"You've got a terminal illness, how old are you ? Growing old is terminal so think about a home for yourself". John the straight talking Tynesider from Gateshead shouted as he tagged on to the edge of the group. Mrs. Gobby scuttled aboard the coach uttering a series of indignant "tuts" followed by her obedient husband.

Eventually Jill and Jenny returned to the coach with Edith, hoping someone had found Georgina. "It's gone six o'clock now". RD shouted as the girls approached. "We can't wait much longer we've still got a good two hour drive to Lucerne". She snapped impatiently. "Well we can't leave her, we can't go until we find her". Jill sniped back. "If you want to go, then bloody well go. Me and Jenny are going back to find a police station, there must be one reasonably close". Jenny raged.

"We'll wait another half an hour, and that's it, if you're not back by seven the coach will go". RD snarled as the girls set off jogging. "You'd better make sure you've got a driver". Jenny turned and shouted as they watched Giovanni racing across the coach park towards them.

"Oh my God, thank goodness". Jill exclaimed on entering the police station and seeing Georgina sat at a desk totally unconcerned chatting to a uniformed policeman.

"Does this lady belong to you ?" The officer asked seeing the relief on their faces. "Where was she ?" Jill enquired, slowly pronouncing every word. "We found her about an hour ago sitting on the kerb with an empty glass. Our officer thought she was drunk so she brought her in to the station". He added

"No she's not drunk, unfortunately she suffers from dementia". Jenny explained. "Yes, we guessed it was something like that, but we were not able to do much because all she could tell us was her name...Georgina. She could not remember her last name or where she was from. We assumed someone would eventually come looking for her".

Jenny and Jill thanked the officer and gleefully lead Georgina back to the coach and into the awaiting arms of Edith, her tearful overjoyed younger sister.

~~~~~~~~~~~~~~~~~

Day five Thursday

The lucky few to be blessed with lakeside balcony rooms woke up to be greeted by the splendour of the dawn sunrise shimmering across the lake. After arriving in Lucerne in darkness and having a late meal, all that the guests were interested in was to get to their allocated rooms and sleep.

The chatter in the dining room at breakfast mainly revolved around the bragging rights of the few guests who were fortunate enough to have been given the best rooms.

"Where's Mavis this morning, she's not gone for a dip in the lake ?" Jenny jokingly asked Joe as he entered the dining room and accepted the girls invitation to sit at their table.

"She won't be coming down, bloody mosquitoes. We made the mistake of opening a window with the light on. You should see her shoulder". Joe spouted. "I don't think she'll be leaving the hotel today, the room's already stifling hot but she won't open the soddin' window again". He added, disappointed at the thought that he ought to keep her company.

"We'll pop up and see her after breakfast, Are you in one of the lake view rooms". Jill asked. "Are we hell....no we're looking onto the hotel next door, we must be above the kitchen, all the waste bins are below us". Joe moaned at his misfortune. "Where are you two girls ?" He asked.

The girls looked at each other with embarrassment as Jill cagily told Joe that they did have one of the lakeside balcony rooms. "Don't be ashamed to tell me, you lucky devils, just enjoy it". He chirped. "One thing for sure, RD couldn't have had anything to do with the distribution of the rooms". Jenny quipped. "We'll be up to see Mavis in a minute, are you taking her some breakfast Joe ?" Jill asked. "Suppose I ought to". Joe replied.

"I'll see how I feel later on, I'm going to get myself back into bed for a couple of hours so you might as well go out Joe. You'll only be a pain in the backside if you hang around here". Mavis said as she winced exposing her shoulder to show Jill and Jenny the red swellings.

"You're very welcome to come along with me and Jenny if you want to Joe, we're only intending to wander around the town this morning". Jill offered. "No, you're alright girls, you go off and enjoy your morning, I'll stay close to the hotel. I'll probably take the dog for a walk along the lake". Joe replied with a mischievous wink.

Jenny's eyes glazed over as she and Jill stared at the array of glittering gold, silver and jewel studded watches on display in the window.

"English". Was Jenny's first word as they entered the shop to be greeted by an immaculately dressed attractive young lady shop assistant smiling from the other side of the glass topped display counter.

"Good morning ladies, yes English is good, are you looking for something special ?" She politely enquired.

The lady assistant unlocked the internal glazed panel and handed Jenny the ladies gold wrist watch that she had identified in the window display. Jenny practically dribbled with excitement as she showed Jill the intricate time piece, hoping it would be within her price range.

"This one is two thousand francs". The sales lady informed Jenny without revealing any emotion or surprise when Jenny said she would take it. "It's approximately sixteen hundred pounds". She added purposely, just so that Jenny fully realised the cost but in a tone of voice so as not to belittle her.

"Yes I know, I've already got some figures in mind". Jenny replied confidently, and then did take the assistant by surprise.

"That's my sister's present sorted now I need one for my dad".

Half an hour later and with just over three thousand pounds worth of gold wrist watches laid on the glass counter glittering in their velvet lined presentation boxes, Jill looked at Jenny as she produced the required amount of Swiss francs from an envelope from her fashionable plastic handbag, all brand new notes banded in five hundred franc packs, and handed them to the sales lady.

"I've given you a five percent reduction for the two watches". She said as she began counting the currency. "It's rather a lot of money to carry around, wouldn't you have preferred to have paid by card ?" The shop lady asked as she handed Jenny her receipt and the relevant paperwork. "I didn't want any problems with the transaction not going through if I'd tried to use my debit card. I hope you don't mind cash". Jenny humbly apologised. "Not at all, you are the customer". She replied "Thank you for your custom, please take care". She added as Jill and Jenny left the shop.

"I think I'll just nip back to our hotel and pop these in to the room safe". Jenny said gripping her handbag tightly. "Yes I think that would be a good idea". Jill answered. "And then let's have a coffee somewhere".

"How's Mavis Joe, is she feeling any better ?" Jill shouted as Joe appeared in the distance. "The hotel gave her some ointment to relieve the stinging. She must be feeling a bit better, we're off on the lake for the afternoon after we've had a bite to eat". Joe replied as he wandered over and waited at the bottom of the hotel's tiled staircase.

"We were just about to have a coffee..... it's half twelve Jill, we might as well have our lunch". Jenny said. "Here's Mavis now, do you feel like something to eat ?" Joe asked his wife as the lift door closed behind her. "Here's me waiting with open arms at the foot of the stairs and she pops out of the bloody lift". Joe joked. "Yes I'm starving, he didn't bring me any breakfast up this morning because he said he thought they might think he was taking it for his lunch". Jenny gave Joe a playful whack across the back of his head with her handbag. "You daft devil". She said affectionately. "

"Anyway why don't we all go and get some lunch together and then spend the afternoon on a boat ride on the lake ?" Mavis asked. "That sounds a lovely idea, I won't be a minute". Jenny said and ignored the waiting lift and noisily clomped up the tiled staircase.

"They're beautiful, look Georgina, look at Jenny's watches". Edith asked her sister as Jenny proudly showed the two expensive gold watches she'd purchased earlier in the day.

"The one is something special...well they both are really. That's for a special thank you to my dad for his birthday present, and the other is for my twin sister when I meet her in Venice. I've still got to find something for my brother". Jenny explained.

"They look expensive, they must have cost you a pretty penny". Edith said cheekily. "Looking at all the others I think I chose the two cheapest watches in the shop. I brought a lot more Swiss francs with me than I would have done especially to get these watches. I wanted to pay in cash so that I made sure there was no problem buying them. I reckon I saved at least two hundred pounds on each watch because of the excellent exchange rate. They're both meant to be surprise presents so I would have been very upset not to have bought them". Jenny proclaimed with satisfaction.

"Where did you get the money to buy those ?" RD screeched as she deliberately strode across the dining room floor from her table to confront Jenny, causing the room to descend into silence and all the guests to stare in amazement. "Mind your own damn business". Jenny flared angrily. "What's it got to do with you ?" She snapped. Jill and the elderly sisters looked on in disbelief.

"I'll tell you what it's got to do with me.......My wallet has been taken from my yellow bag sometime when we arrived here in the dark last night, and you two were the last to get off the coach. I always leave the bag on the cill at the front. I keep my money and my passport in it. No I haven't lost it, I've already searched everywhere I can think of". RD bawled convincingly.

Gasps of bewilderment and 'Oh my God's' were heard around the room, and the noise level returned with the prospect that an angry scene was about to explode.

Jenny jumped to her feet and stood eyeball to chin in a mismatched face off.

"Why accuse Jenny, anybody could have taken it". Jill screamed at the same time joining Jenny at her side in support.

"I don't see anyone else flashing three thousand quids worth of watches around". RD bellowed for everyone within a couple of miles to hear, causing the hotel manager to enter the fray. "This is just another of your vicious attempts to victimise me and Jill. For some reason you've hated us from the first day you saw us, you old bag". Jenny snarled unable to resist the insult. "I think we should take this into my office, stop your shouting and come with me ladies". The hotel manager implored in perfect English. "Please carry on and enjoy your meal". He requested the room full of guests as the noise level began to increase again.

"Please calm down, take a seat". He instructed as Jenny burst into uncontrollable sobbing. "I'll have to pop back, I've left my watches on the table". She said through a succession of sniffles. "I'll go". Jill uttered and swiftly returned with the watches safely in her hand having run the gauntlet of a few jeering diners

"I want the police to be called". RD insisted menacingly. "Wait a moment". Urged the manager, a neatly fashionably dressed tall slim dark haired thirtyish gentleman in an immaculate charcoal grey suit and matching waist coat.

RD then persuasively explained the reason why she would have so much money in Swiss francs in her wallet unattended. That it was to get her through until the winter season when she would return to Switzerland to work. "That's as maybe, but it doesn't mean I took it". Jenny screeched storming back on the attack.

"I deliberately brought a lot of Swiss francs with me solely with the intention of buying a Swiss watch for my sister and one for my dad's birthday. I'm not a thief". She screamed emphatically.

"Have you anyway to prove you purchased your francs ?" The manager quietly asked Jenny. "Do you still have your exchange rate receipt ?" He added enquiringly.

"No unfortunately I don't. I just put all my Swiss money in an envelope to keep it separate specially to buy the watches".

"And how about you Miss Devlin, do you have proof as to how you come to have over three thousand pounds worth of francs". The manager asked turning his attention to RD.

"I've saved it, I worked all through the winter season in charge of a ski chalet, and it's what I've saved from my earnings. I have to put money aside to get me through the rest of the year. I can't always find another job, I was very lucky finding this courier vacancy. I only got it because they were stuck at the last minute". RD replied plausibly.

"Well all I can suggest for the moment is for you to report your wallet to the police as missing and hope you've just mislaid it somewhere. I can not see that you can go round accusing anyone, you have no reason to suspect this young lady". The manager advised to RD's indignant look of dissatisfaction.

"If you telephone the Bureau de Change I used I'm sure they would be able to confirm that I bought this amount of Swiss francs". Jenny said, interrupting RD before she was about to have another outburst.

"Don't bother, but everybody in the

coach knows that you took it". RD snarled vengefully.

"That is enough........ now go back to your tables and I will organise some fresh meals for you". He generously instructed.

RD immediately stormed from the office and strutted triumphantly back to her table. Jenny and Jill politely declined the offer of a fresh meal, instead preferring to return to their room, this giving the impression that the girls were somehow guilty of the theft.

~~~~~~~~~~~~~~~~~

Day six Friday

The next morning Jill and Jenny decided to miss breakfast to avoid the hostility and humiliation created against them by RD. Jenny spent the first couple of hours, firstly contacting the Bureau de Change without success and then her own bank. The latter after extensive identity checks, although fully appreciating her predicament were unwilling to forward a copy of her current bank statement by email, but they did confirm the existence of the transaction with the Bureau de Change, and they added that a statement had been sent to her home address two days earlier.

"I do hope dad hasn't gone away yet, I know he's off to be with a mate sometime while I'm away". Jenny groaned as she waited anxiously listening to the dialling tone.

"Dad". She shrieked as he answered. "Jenny, what's up ?" "I've got a bit of a problem". Jenny started and proceeded to relate the situation she was in. "What can I do ?" Her dad asked. "Is there any mail for me ?" Jenny asked with butterflies cramping her chest. "Just the one, looks like it's from your bank". Dad assumed by the reverse side of the envelope. "Can you open it...is it a statement ?" Jenny urged.

A moment, which seemed like an age to Jenny, passed while he removed the document from the envelope. "Come on dad, is it ?" Jenny butted in. "Yes, what do you want to know ?" "Look at the last few items is there a cheque payment to the Bureau de Charge for nearly four thousand pounds". Jenny asked with her breath held. Dad confirmed the transaction.

"Do you know how to scan it on to the laptop ? Oh God I didn't think you would". Jenny sighed at his brief reply. "But Jakey next door isn't at school today, I've seen him in the back garden. Leave it with me I'll ask him, he'll know how to do it. How's your holiday going anyway ?" He chirped. "Never mind about the holiday, tell you all about that later....After he's scanned it ask him to email to me. My number is in the book. Do it now dad, please it's urgent". Jenny cried and hung up.

"Oh God I hope he manages to get the kid from next door to get it right. All I can do is wait". Jenny said after telling Jill the gist of the conversation she'd just completed with her father.

Jenny sighed with relief that her dad was still at home and now took a few moments to relax with the knowing that hopefully she would soon have the information to prove her innocence.

During Jenny's lengthy conversation, Jill nipped out to a nearby delicatessen and returned with a couple of filled rolls to substitute missing breakfast.

"I know what I'll do. I'll have the evil bitch, We'll be first down to dinner tonight and wait until the dining room's full, and then I'll stuff my statement up her bloody nose and demand an apology in front of the whole hotel. I don't believe that she's even lost her wallet, and if she has, I doubt if there was much money in it ?" Jenny ranted.

"When it comes through why don't you show it to the hotel manager instead, and ask him if he would mention it in the dining room during dinner when everybody is present". Jill suggested. Jenny agreed to this alternative, knowing her nerves would most certainly let her down in an open conflict in front of an audience..

For the next ten minutes Jenny's eyes were glued to the two inch square mobile phone screen and screamed with glee when the email appeared, and quickly opened the attachment in her inbox to reveal the statement she'd been waiting for.

"Look Jill". Jenny screamed as she pushed her phone in front of Jill's face. "Right then, let's go and find the manager, you coming with me Jill". Jenny added with her pulse racing at double it's intended rate.

The two girls bounced down the tiled staircase and leaned breathlessly on the reception desk.

"Is it possible for us to see the hotel manager please ?" Jenny excitedly asked the young lady behind the desk.

"I'm afraid he is not here at the moment but I'll tell him the minute he arrives. Who shall I say wants to see him ?" The receptionist replied. At that precise moment the hotel manager walked through the door.

"Mateo....these two young ladies wish to see you". "Is there another problem ladies ?" He enquired. "No just the opposite. I contacted my bank and they had sent out my statement to my home, so my dad has emailed it to my phone. And if you look you can see there that I paid a cheque to Bureau de Charge on the twenty ninth of July for three thousand eight hundred and eighty two pounds and forty eight pence". Jenny chirped thrilled at the thought of putting RD in her place as she held out her phone for the manager to see.

"I was wondering if you would be prepared to speak on my behalf at dinner tonight, so that the guests know that I didn't steal that money". Jenny asked hopefully.

"Much as I sympathise with you, I could not possibly humiliate another hotel guest, so I am afraid you must deal with the situation yourself. I have no objection if you stand on a table and shout it from the roof tops. But do not tell anyone I said that, and do not tell me if you intend to do that". He said quietly with a broad smile on his face.

"What do you two want ?" RD snarled at Jill and Jenny as they arrived at her table after weaving their way between the tables of disapproving diners.

"Just to show you this". Jenny said and thrust her phone within a few inches of RD's face. "What's this then ?" RD snapped. "It's a copy of my current bank statement and there's the proof that I didn't steal your money, that's assuming you did lose your wallet". Jenny said controlling her simmering temper for a moment, that was until RD ignored and sneered at her and turned her back and carried on eating her meal.

Then Jenny began an angry outburst. "So now you can come and stand in the middle of the room and apologise to me in front of all these hotel guests, or if you don't I'll jump up on a table and tell everyone myself what a spiteful vindictive woman you are".

"Alright, so all it proves is that you bought a lot of currency, but it still doesn't prove you didn't take my wallet". RD replied defiantly.

With no sign of RD complying with her demand and Jenny not having the courage to carry out her threat, she nervously wandered throughout the dining room with her phone in hand, chatting to all the guests individually in the hope of convincing them of her innocence.

After half an hour with Jill in tow for moral support, the girls settled down besides Edith and Georgina and could now put aside RD's accusation and enjoy their evening meal, suitably satisfied that the majority of guests were now on their side.

RD sat staring hard at the blank wall to avoid the gaze of the other diners. Her short mousey brown hair revealed her bare neck visibly growing pinker by the minute. To add to her embarrassment Joe and steelworker John simultaneously stood at their tables and began to applaud Jenny, and were soon joined in the clapping by several of the diners adding more colour to RD's ever reddening neck and face.

"Well done Jen, we knew you hadn't taken her money......now then, who did". Joe said and whispered with the back of his hand across his mouth. "That's If anybody did". "Now then who did ?" Joe added sinisterly. "Someone on the coach.....but who, send for Helical Spiral". He joked recreating a spoof Agatha Christie mystery for the remainder of the holiday.

The evening entertainment of dancing in the hotel lounge provided some much needed relief for Jill and Jenny and they found themselves the constant target for the more able gentlemen in the group wishing to show off their prowess at the cha cha and after a few drinks, their versions of the jive.

"You're good". Joe praised the girls. "I'd have thought you two would be into the disco dancing not ballroom". Joe added as he and Mavis returned to their seats. "We like both, we go to the night club in town once a week, don't we Jill". Jenny quipped. "Mind you we both prefer a nice romantic waltz with some handsome bloke who can really dance". Jenny said as she stood to partner Jill for a square tango. "We know this....come on Mave". Joe chirped hauling his wife to her feet.

"I'm your man if they play a romantic waltz". Joe joked. "You'll dance with me if they do, you old flirt, stand up straight and stop fooling around". Mavis laughed as she dragged Joe back into line and placed his hands into dance hold.

Jill and Jenny completed a successful evening sitting in the darkness on their hotel balcony sipping a glass of wine and watching the party atmosphere from the outside bar below and the fireflies zipping around the street lights.

~~~~~~~~~~~~~~~

Day seven Saturday

RD was on full throttle as she held the microphone hard against her mouth in pop star fashion, "Today ladies and gentlemen we're taking a short trip to Interlaken where we will spend the next three nights. We should arrive by twelve so you have the rest of the day free to explore the area or take a trip on the lake". She announced, although at full volume, but sounding more like the professional courier she is meant to be.

"Tomorrow some of you are going on the organised excursion to the Schilthorn. If anyone else wishes to come along, it's a fantastic day out. This will cost you about sixty pounds with your Swiss pass. You can get a lunch in the revolving restaurant where a James Bond scene was made. So if you're interested see me during the journey".

"What are you doing about your missing money Rose ?" Joe shouted out mischievously. RD began to flush slightly and gave Joe the look of a witch casting a spell for asking such an obviously bated question which she would have probably preferred to ignore. She inserted the microphone almost inside her mouth to make a further announcement, then lowering the microphone, and in an unusual softer tone of voice informed Joe and anyone else who was listening that for the time being she had just reported it as missing to the police in Lucerne.

"And the day after". She said and momentarily paused, and then burst into full volume with the microphone pressed against her lips. "We have the highlight of your holiday, a trip to the top of the Jungfrau mountain". "Jungfraujoch". Dug the bug corrected in his childish irritating manner. "Whatever". RD snarled angrily at the rude interruption and continued. "The train takes you through the inside of the Eiger to the highest point in Europe. I've never been myself so I'm looking forward to it.

Anyway, as we're in a mixture of hotels in Interlaken we'll all meet at the railway station at ten o'clock. It's ten o'clock at the station tomorrow for the Schilthorn as well". RD concluded.

"Der Bahnhof". Duggie shouted, unable to resist giving everyone the benefit of his knowledge of his German interpretation for the railway station, which he'd probably just looked up in his guide book. "Bahnhof yourself". RD screeched at him, gaining herself a few brownie points for putting him in his place.

With just the girls, two other couples and RD remaining, the coach drew into the hotel car park for the last passenger drop off.

"This is your hotel folks". RD bellowed with a sadistic sneer of satisfaction. The use of the microphone being slightly unnecessary. "I'll just pop inside and make sure everything is ready for you". RD smugly chirped at the prospect of knowingly leaving her six most hated guests at the worst accommodation.

A very drab modern building, lacking any characteristics of the area, empty at this time of the year and used mainly as winter apartments.

"A buffet breakfast is available in the bar but you'll have to go to the Hotel Gloriana for your evening meal". RD delighted in telling the six as Giovanni handed each their luggage.

The culprits being the obvious six, Joe and his wife Mavis. Ex marine and steel worker John and Lucy, his lady companion, and of course the two she hates most of all, the teenage girls, Jill and Jenny.

"It looks as if we've got to carry our own luggage, oh well let's go and see what the rooms are like". John the old soldier chirped as he lifted a suitcase in each hand and marched into the deserted reception lobby followed by Joe with Mavis tagging behind dragging her wheelie suitcase.

"This place is empty, there's nobody around to ask anything". John moaned as no one appeared after he rang the bell for the fourth time.

"Those must be our room keys" Jill assumed, pointing to a wooden tray on the counter. "Well this one says Smith". Joe announced with a sneaky wink at Mavis. "That's us". John answered. "These must be yours Jenny". Joe added and he passed the keys around.

"They don't intend you walking away with these, the key fob weighs a ton. I think I'll go and put the key in the door and come back down for cases, I doubt if I can manage to carry both at the same time". John joked and added.. "The demon woman knew what she was doing dropping us off at this dump".

"Well I suppose we'd better go and see if we can find our rooms in this God forsaken hole". Joe grunted while they all stood waiting with their luggage at the lift door.

"At least we're all on the same floor.....I think, that's if the key numbers have anything to do with it". Joe moaned again.

"This looks like a large bedsit, we've got a kitchen area and a massive lounge space. The beds drop out of the wall". Jill gasped with disgust as she observed the many stains on the biscuit coloured slightly threadbare rug which covered the lounge area. "Stupid thing to have on the floor in a place like this anyway".

"Dirty devils". Jill retorted when she saw the state of the kitchen floor tiles. "Is there a mop and bucket in one of those cupboards ?" She asked. "These cupboards are all locked and it says not to be used and the cooker's taped up. Oh.....this cupboard's open, there's a hoover and an ironing board in here and spare toilet rolls, that's all. You wouldn't get these marks off, not without getting on your hands and knees with scouring pads. I hate to think what the bathroom is like, do we have our own ? I bloody hope so. At least they've left us a kettle and a couple of mugs. They want scolding out though before they can be used".

Jenny tugged at the thick cord to open up one of the two wall mounted beds. "The bed looks clean, thank God". She said as she removed the binding straps and threw back the duvet. "All looks nicely pressed fresh linen, this one's mine". She chirped.

"This bed's clean as well, they must use a different person to change the beds to the one who cleans the room". Jill proclaimed and began to hoist the bed back into it's daytime position. "This place must be meant for groups of lads or girls, it's no place for privacy if you were a couple". Jill added.

"What's that on the floor Jill ? It just dropped from the wall when you pushed the bed back". "It's a wallet". Jill replied. "Don't pick it up Jill". Jenny screeched. "Use a tissue. The cunning vicious cow. She must have nipped up to our room when Giovanni was getting our luggage out of the coach and stuffed it into the side of the bed". Jenny cursed.

"There's nothing in it, it could be anybody's". Jill stated after carefully looking inside. "No it's her's alright, it's too much of a coincidence, and it's red plastic" Jenny snarled.

"I reckon the police will be here in ten minutes, so let's go out and take it with us. The demon woman won't expect us to have found it yet, or if we had she'd think we'd get caught with it. First chance we get we'll sneak it back in her yellow bag. That'll have her guessing". Jenny chuntered.

"What's your room like ?". Joe groaned to the girls as he met them on his way down the polished concrete staircase. "It's a bit impersonal, in fact it's horrible". Jill moaned. "Yes, ours is bloody awful as well. I didn't think we had a bed, but we've got two, they come out of the wall. I was just going to see if I could find someone to ask when Mavis showed me where it was".

"Are you going out?" Joe asked the girls. "Yes, we're just going to have a wander to see what the town's like and then we thought we'd have a walk to the lake". Jill answered.

"Mavis will be down in a minute, when she's finished putting her walking out head on. Here she is now. Would you mind if we tagged along?" Joe asked in his usual jocular manner as Jenny stood impatiently looking towards the street for any signs of a police vehicle. "Yes of course you can come with us, let's go". Jenny urged.

"What do you think of Interlaken?" Mavis asked the girls when they returned to within a hundred yards of their hotel. "Not a lot, it's about as inspiring as our accommodation". Jill replied then slyly nudged Jenny nervously as they watched a police car turn into their hotel car park.

"Did you see that? A police car just went to our hotel, I wonder what they're after". Mavis pondered. "They've probably come for John for abducting young girls". Joe said inappropriately as his joke back fired. ""You mustn't say things like that, your big mouth will get you in trouble one of these days. Lucy is in her late sixties and John told me he'll be eighty three in a couple of weeks. So watch those stupid jokes you make". Mavis lectured. "That's me told". Joe retorted in an attempt to overcome his slight embarrassment at being reprimanded by his wife.

"We've got a long time to kill, we can't stare at the lake forever, there's a boat coming in, shall we have a ride to where ever it's going next". Joe suggested as someone with a squeaky voice called out "Thun".

"Oh hello Heather, you two off on the lake ? Which hotel are you in ?" Jill asked. "We're in with the demon at the Gloriana, it's a lovely hotel. What's yours like ?" Heather enquired. "Bloody lousy". Joe jumped in. "No, ours isn't very nice, we're in some sort of winter ski apartments, I think. The place is completely deserted, there's only the six of us there. We've got to come to your hotel for our dinner tonight". Jill moaned.

Douglas wandered along the side of the boat writing something in his notepad while at the same time getting in the way of a couple of disembarking tourists.

"It's going to go in a minute, are we getting on". Mavis urged. "Well there's bugger all to do here". Joe coarsely replied.

"How lovely". Mavis gushed as after twenty minutes into the ride the boat veered to stop at a jetty and a happy wedding party including the bride and her six bridesmaids all in traditional white dresses joined the boat. "Are you just off to be married or have you just got married ?" Joe cheekily asked the slim elegant attractive girl in the bridal dress. "Wie bitte". The girl replied. "English, no" Joe asked, answering himself.

"She's on her way to be married in Thun". One of the bridesmaids interjected, and then explained to the future bride what Joe had asked.

The would be bride smiled back at Joe's smiling face and invited the four of them to join in the on board pre-wedding reception party. "She says you are all very welcome to to stay and have a drink with us". The bridesmaid translated acting as the interpreter.

"He always manages to embarrass me, fancy asking that young girl that. He can't stop flirting, mind you he's got the sort of smile that can charm the birds from the trees. I suppose that's why I fell for him". Mavis said. "Look at him now, right in amongst the bridesmaids chatting away ten to the dozen. They can't understand a word he's saying. Daft as a brush". Mavis gasped exasperated.

Within moments she was flattered to find herself deep in conversation and being handed a glass of white wine by a very handsome, smartly dressed Swiss gentleman.

In the meantime two of the younger members of the party boldly sidled up to Jill and Jenny with a tray of drinks and very politely introduced themselves.

"We're going to watch the wedding". Mavis informed the girls as they stepped from the boat. "So are we". Laughed Jenny. "We're going to follow them to the church, the wedding is at three. It's twenty five to now". Jenny uttered.

"The Baggies don't have a match today". Joe blurted for no reason out of the blue. "Oh shut up Joe, no one wants to know that". Mavis scolded her husband. "Who are the Baggies ?" Jenny chuckled with amusement. "It's his football team, West Bromwich Albion". Mavis groaned in an effort to stem that particular topic of conversation.

"This is turning out to be the best day of the holiday". Mavis chirped as she and Joe and the girls graciously accepted the invitation to attend the wedding reception on the return boat ride. "Jill and Jenny look as if they're enjoying themselves, they've got a good looking fella each". She gushed.

"Isn't this where you caught the boat". Jill asked Isaac, her young Swiss male suitor. "Yes but we are all going on to Interlaken for the main evening reception at the Hotel Gloriana. You and Jenny must come". "We can't intrude any more...can we ?" Jill replied hopeful for a positive answer.

"You will come ! You are all invited as my guests to our sister's wedding". Axel demanded in no uncertain terms. "Well we can't refuse an invitation like that, can we Mave". Joe muttered.

"So you two are brothers then ?" Jenny butted in. "Yes, we are twins, obviously not identical twins". Isaac quipped. "You were keeping that a secret". Jenny gulped at the coincidence.

"That's strange, I'm a twin as well, I've got a twin sister, she lives in America, and me and Jill are sort of twins we share the same birthday, we're nineteen. How old are you ?"

"Twenty". Isaac replied. "And how old are you Axel ?" Joe asked keeping a straight face. Axel looked at Joe a bit bemused by the question. "He's joking with you Axel, take no notice. You are joking I hope". Mavis retorted displaying her annoyance.

"Tell them about your dog Joe". Jill sniggered with her mischievous request and burst into laughter at her thoughts". "For goodness sake Jill, don't egg him on. Joe....don't you dare". Mavis threatened with gritted teeth.

"So you have a twin sister in America and you and Jill were also born on the same day". Mavis gulped in amazement. Followed by a lengthy explanation from Jenny about her family history and her excitement at her arranged meeting with her sister when they go on the excursion to Venice.

"RD and her group of favourites staying at the Gloriana are in for a surprise when they see us four arrive. I hope they've not gone out". Joe said gleefully.

"We'll meet you there". Joe shouted as he and Mavis remained with the wedding party and strolled the short distance to the hotel, while Jill and Jenny accompanied by their new boy friends called in at their accommodation for the girls to change into something more appropriate.

"Is this where you have to stay, it's disgusting". Axel commented. But Jill and Jenny were too engrossed in looking for signs that they had been visited by the police to listen to him continuing to rant about the condition of the room. "I'd forgotten all about them all afternoon, Well if they have been in, they've not disturbed anything". Jill whispered. "They have been here, I didn't leave my bag on the chair". Jenny remarked. "Who cares....turn your backs you two while we change". Jill instructed their young Swiss friends.

RD and several couples from their tour gulped on their drinks with open mouths as Jill and Jenny dressed to kill in their beautiful evening gowns, boastfully paraded past, arm in arm with their respective Swiss boy friends and on into the private ballroom reserved for the wedding party.

"I made a deliberate point of chatting to the old demon witch. She delighted in telling me we were too late for dinner. I told her she could stick her dinner...you know where, and marched in here". Joe gloated and laughed loudly.

The girls were handed glasses of champagne and introduced and embraced by the bride and groom and their boyfriend's parents the moment they stepped into the room, together with lots of eye popping from the gentlemen present.

"Well that was a good start, our mother and father like you, mind you, our father did comment on how nice you seemed when he saw us all together outside the church". Axel said as he prised Jenny's hand from his father's grip.

.

The bride and her new tall handsome husband beckoned their guests onto the dance floor as they smooched around the room to the strains of Moon River being excellently played by a five piece orchestra, with the lyrics sweetly sung by a glamorous lady vocalist.

Isaac, now like most of the men folk, minus his immaculate tailored jacket, but still looking very dapper and handsome in his navy blue waistcoat, lead Jill on to the ballroom floor, closely followed by Axel and Jenny.

"What's this, I don't know this dance ?" Jenny asked anxiously as the fast tempo of the music began. "It's a polka". Isaac called out from a few feet away. "I've never done this either". Jill uttered and tried in vain to pull Isaac to the side of the floor.

"Can you waltz ?" Isaac asked staring at Jill with his deep blue eyes. "Yes...but". "Then dance the waltz but a bit quicker with a lot of twirling". After a couple of false starts the two couples laughed their way around the large ballroom floor.

The evening seemed to fly by all too fast for the girls, thinking this was now the end of a very brief holiday romance.

"What a night Mave, it's been awhile since we danced till two in the morning". Joe chirped, now slightly more sober than an hour ago. "We've never danced till two in the morning, and it's only just gone twelve you silly sod". Mavis responded. "I wonder how the Albion got on". "Oh shut up Joe, you said they weren't playing so there's no need for the miseries for another week...they can't have lost". Mavis said as her patience started to wane.

"Jill and Jenny kept dancing all evening, I don't know where they get the energy, I'm absolutely shattered. They look a bit sad at the moment. It looks as though Jenny has been crying, and Jill doesn't look too happy. I think they've fallen for those lads". Mavis observed sympathetically as she attempted to disguise a yawn.

"No, you stay here in the hotel with your family, me and Jill will be fine. It's best if we say goodbye here, it's only a few hundred yards to our place, we've got a key in case it's been locked up". Jenny sighed with a trace of tears appearing in the corner of her eyes.

With their jackets loosely draped over their shoulders, Isaac and Axel ignored Jenny's disheartened request and followed the two girls out into the warm night air.

"I said we will be alright". Jenny repeated rather unconvincingly. "And I said we will see you back to your hotel". Isaac ordered as the girls resistance easily dwindled away as they set off slightly intoxicated hand in hand along the deserted street.

"This is us then, I suppose you two fellas will be looking for a new girl friend each tomorrow". Jill uttered in an effort to ease the sorrow she was feeling.

"Goodnight you youngsters". Joe and Mavis called out in unison, surprised that the front door was partially open and an elderly male attendant was stood leaning on the desk reading the daily paper.

"Is the Albion score in there mate ?" Joe joked. "For God's sake Joe give it a bloody rest. They didn't soddin' play". Mavis scorned as she watched him deep in conversation in a language he didn't understand as the lift door closed.

"What are you girls doing tomorrow ?" Axel asked with the hopeful expectation of an invite. "We've booked on the organised trip to go to the Schilthorn for the day". Jill sighed at the thought that if they hadn't, and were free the boys might have asked to take them out.

"Can me and Isaac come along with you". Axel enquired. "That would be lovely but it's a trip with the tour and we've already paid for the train fare and the cable cars". Jenny replied, also quite annoyed that they could have had another day with their Swiss friends.

"What time is your train ?" Axel asked. "We've been told to be at the station for ten". Jenny uttered. "That is settled then...we will be here to meet you at nine forty five, it is only ten minutes walk to the bahnhof". Axel responded

"No one can stop us coming with you as long as we pay for ourselves". Isaac added.

After several minutes of saying goodnight, Jill and Jenny floated on air as they ignored the open door of the lift and dreamily climbed the polished staircase.

Meantime Isaac an Axel wandered on cloud nine back to the Hotel Gloriana.

~~~~~~~~~~~~~~~~

Day eight Sunday

My God, we're getting some filthy looks from RD and her cronies". Jill exclaimed. "I think we're beginning to get under her skin, especially if the police told her they didn't find anything in our room. She's now wondering whether they missed it or if we've got it. She's put herself in a bit of a mess, she can't very well ask us if we found it and she can't go back to the police and tell them where to find it". Jill added with a deep satisfying intake of air.

"We can't afford to be seen with it, we need to get it back into her bag as soon as possible. I told Axel all about her last night, so he's holding on to it at the moment. He thinks we're being a bit foolish. If we get caught putting it back we'll be in serious trouble, and if we do put it back, she'll obviously know it was us and can easily plant it on us again. He says we should get rid of it for good", Jenny remarked.

"I think I agree with him Jenny, she'll wonder forever whether it's still in that bed, where do you reckon we dump it ?". Jill asked. "Axel said he'll get rid of it". Jenny answered.

"Look at the demon creature now, she's furious that we've got the boys along for company, she hasn't said anything yet, just keeps giving us daggers. I reckon she'll explode any moment". Jenny said and smiled in

RD's direction as she deliberately cuddled up to Axel.

"Here it comes". Jill chuntered as the woman in the large red uniform jumped from her seat and marched the few yards and stood menacingly staring at the Swiss lads. "This carriage is for Red Demon Tours only". She barked at the lads sitting besides Jill and Jenny. "I am sorry to disappoint you Fräulein, but this is a scheduled Swiss rail journey and nowhere does it say any carriages are reserved for anyone. It is not even a first class carriage. Why do you not try and throw those two couples out if you can". Isaac said politely and calmly, indicating with his eyes towards the other strangers in the carriage, causing RD to huff and puff her way back to her seat.

"Have you not thought to report her to her company for the way she treats people ? Is it just you two ? Have you been on a tour with her before ?" Axel asked Jenny in quick succession.

"We haven't reported her but someone has, she probably thinks it's us. She doesn't treat anybody properly, but us and Joe and Mavis seem to come off the worst. Joe and Mavis and John and Lucy get it in the neck because they've become our friends, and Joe couldn't give a damn what he says".

"We don't know much about you and Axel, we told you all about our lives last night". Jill chirped. "Well at the moment we are both taking two weeks holiday, we only got out of the army last Thursday. Otherwise we live at home with our parents. We have another brother and two sisters. You met them all yesterday, our eldest sister was the one who got married and our other sister was the bridesmaid who translated for her. Our parents have never learned to speak English either. We all work as a family running our hotel and the farm". Isaac responded proudly.

"You mean to say you have your own hotel and you held the reception at someone else's hotel". Jenny blurted in astonishment as she turned her head to the rear to face Isaac and Jill.

"We do not have the facilities in our hotel to cater for a function as big as our sister's wedding. We do not have a room big enough for that number to dine or to dance and we have no where near enough bedrooms to accommodate all the guests who wanted to stay overnight. Anyway it is only money, our parents can afford it.......We do have a few other hotels scattered around Europe though, but not close enough to have used last night". Isaac added without elaborating or any feeling of embarrassment.

"Lauterbrunnen". Shouted the guard as the train came to a halt. "This is it ladies". Isaac, ever the gentleman politely remarked and assisted Jill from the train, followed just as gallantly by Axel and Jenny to the envy of RD and the most of the women in the party.

A cable car and a further train ride

delivered the group to the village of Murren. Jill and Jenny and their Swiss companions decided to stop for an open air coffee overlooking the majestic three peaks, Monch, Jungfrau and the Eiger. To their annoyance they were immediately joined by RD and two couples.

"She's here again, wherever we go she deliberately follows us to try to intimidate us". Jill sighed quietly as the red vision and four of her crones shuffled their chairs into position on the next table. "She thinks she's frightening us". Jenny whispered. "She does frighten me, I wouldn't want to be left alone with her". Jill replied with a cupped hand over her mouth.

"Where is your tour going when you leave Interlaken ?" Axel asked. "We stop at Stressa for three nights, I think we visit Verona and then Florence for two or three nights then some seaside town, and the last day we have a stop in Sorrrento for a few hours before we go on to Naples to catch our flight". Jill said very informatively. "Do we ?" Jenny gasped at Jill's attention to the itinerary.

"Me and Isaac have been thinking, we are still on holiday so when we get back to Interlaken if you and Jill grab you bags from your hotel and come with us and stay at our hotel tonight, we have a couple of spare rooms. Then tomorrow we will go by car to meet the train and join your party at Lauterbrunnen. Then after we have been up the Jungfraujoch we can set off and drive through Italy and meet up again with your tour at Naples airport". Axel suggested hopefully, taking the girls totally by surprise.

It took several seconds before the girls could respond as they stared at each other across the table. "Are you serious ? It sounds an absolutely lovely idea but we couldn't afford to pay for more hotels, we've already paid for this tour". Jill said sounding slightly disappointed at having to decline a wonderful dream.

RD and her four cohorts on the adjacent table sat wide eyed and in complete silence listening intently to their conversation. RD's curiosity snapped and she found it impossible to resist the urge to interfere.

"If you leave the party you won't be allowed back to catch the flight, you'll have broken your contracts with the company". RD screeched, arousing the rest of the cafe diners and loud enough for the whole of Murren to hear.

"I just said we can't afford to anyway, so keep your nose out of our business". Jill snarled back in anger.

"Take no notice of her, of course you still have your flight home, you have paid for it. She is wrong, she can not stop you using your airline ticket. In any case it is only money, me and Isaac will sort that side of things, it will not cost you a cent. And if you are worried about hotel costs we will take our tents". Axel advised with reference to the tents intended as a joke.

"And she can not stop you going on the

trip tomorrow either, you have already paid for that as well. We will meet your group on the train at Lauterbrunnen in the morning". Axel added willing the girls to accept his and Isaac's proposal while staring with menacing determination at RD.

Jenny looked at Jill despondently. "What do you reckon Jill... Shall we ?" "Well anything's better than this torment and another week with this bat and some of the obnoxious sods on the coach". Jenny gushed. "Bugger it...why not. But we will pay our own way. We're okay for spending money and we will settle up with you when we get home". Jill squealed with delight.

"I suppose it's my money you'll be spending". RD grunted with a gesture of waving her arms frantically in despair at the excited girls reactions at accepting the Swiss lads offer.

"Oh stop being a pathetic old witch and put a sock in it. We've gone through all this before, you know we didn't take your wallet you stupid woman". Jenny said forcefully causing a smile on both the lads faces.

Isaac looked at Jenny slightly bemused. "Put a sock in it. What does that mean ?" He quizzed. "Never mind, I'll explain later. Come on let's have a walk and get the cable car up to the Schilthorn. Let's leave this demon woman and her friends to their misery. I've had enough of her". Jenny bawled.

"Your very best friend is down there". Axel joked, pointing to the external platform below. covered in a layer of fresh snow and glistening in the warmth of the midday sun. "She's still there". Jill observed as the revolving restaurant completed one revolution. "The size of her in that ridiculous red uniform is probably visible from outer space, especially against the snow". Jenny bitched. "A good push over the rail is what she needs to complete our holiday". Jill chirped. "Forget her, your holiday starts now, are we all having dessert?" Isaac asked and produced a couple of menus.

"So it is all settled, you stay with us at our parent's hotel tonight and in the morning we will drive to Lauterbrunnen to catch the train. Then after we have done the Jungfrau we will set off and make our own route and drive down through Italy, so say bye, bye to your friendly tour guide".

"I feel sorry for Joe and Mavis, we've become great friends with them. They're such a funny couple, we never know if they're kidding". Jill said sorrowfully. "What is kidding?" Axel enquired. "Oh it's just word for making something up". Jill answered.

During lunch in the revolving restaurant Jenny explained the situation regarding her twin sister and her half brother including the devastation her mother caused her father when she left him and went to live in America with another man. "We must visit Venice next Wednesday, I've arranged to meet my sister and my brother there. They're on a world cruise with my mum and her second husband. They dock in Venice for just the one night, so we must be there that day". Jenny demanded. "This was the only reason we chose The Red Demon tour because it was the only one I could find that had an excursion to Venice at the right time". She added. "That's no bother, we will stay somewhere close by, we will make sure you get to meet them". Isaac assured.

One final photograph taken of the four, Jill, Jenny, Isaac and Axel completed Mavis's session.

"I must have one of Joe and Mavis with both of us, I probably won't get another chance". Jill chirped and handed her camera to Isaac. "Now can I have one of just me sandwiched between the girls". Joe suggested. "Go on then". Mavis laughed and retrieved her camera from her handbag. "That is definitely the last photo". She added.

"We will see you tomorrow, won't we ?" Mavis asked sincerely. "Yes, we are coming tomorrow, we'll see you on the train at Lauterbrunnen in the morning". Jill uttered.

"We're going to get off now Mavis". Jenny said softly. "Come here you two". Joe quipped and gave both girls a kiss on both cheeks. "You'll see them again tomorrow, he can't help himself, he's nothing but an outrageous flirt". Mavis snapped. "Oh good, I'll have another kiss tomorrow as well then".

"Come on you two". Isaac called out from the lake back in Interlaken, to Jenny and Axel as they dawdled along locked together with their arms around each other's waist.

Jenny's wheelie case weaving in all directions being dragged along by Axel with his free hand.

"Here we are then". Axel retorted as the lake boat pulled alongside the pier. "And here is our transport". He added seeing his father proudly leaning on his gleaming 1950's Rolls Royce.

"He bought this car in nineteen seventy four in this condition, it has never had a bump. Except for the shape it still looks brand new". Isaac informed the girls as they shuffled around in the luxurious soft leather comfort of the rear seats. "He will never part with it, will you vati. He is as daft as a broom, that is a Mavis expression. He is smiling, pretending to know what I said". Axel said returning his father's smile. "The expression is daft as a brush, not broom". Jenny corrected.

The rolls purred through a tiny village at ten miles per hour. "This is as fast as he ever drives around here, mind you it is as fast as he ever does drive because he never drives it anywhere else. Only joking he uses it as a taxi to collect guests from the airport". Axel said. "This is our little village, and this is our hotel". Axel added as the two tone maroon and cream vehicle came to a halt in front of an oversize weathered oak door.

Jill swiftly jumped from the car and immediately began to take photographs of the charming traditional Swiss chalet nestling gently on a sloping meadow overlooking the three mountain peaks, their destination for the following day.

"Everything here seems to be typically Swiss". Jill noted after enjoying the evening meal. "Well our parents realised a long time ago that it is what the foreign guests come for. The building, the views, the food and our local entertainment. Tonight it is a couple of village lads, they are very good. "Isaac chirped as he and Jill wandered out on to the terrace to watch the sun set.

~~~~~~~~~~~~~~~~

Day nine Monday

Isaac watched admiringly from the timbered balcony at the two girls in the distance strolling across an open meadow knee deep in fresh moist grass, adorned with an assortment of colourful wild flowers.

"Did you not sleep very well ? It is not eight o'clock yet". He shouted to the girls as they entered the coolness of the long shadow cast by the hotel, both dressed in jeans and sweaters.

"Yes, we had a good night, we woke up too early, it's a beautiful morning so we went for a walk to find your animals. I thought you said that you had a farm". Jenny shouted back with pretence sarcasm. .

"No, they are on the higher slopes at the moment. You would not see them, they will be coming down into the barns soon". Isaac replied as he reached the ground floor rear entrance to greet the girls and to give Jill a kiss on her lips before explaining fully the workings of the farm.

"Anyway breakfast is ready, we will eat in the guest's dining room this morning, are you hungry after your walk ?" Isaac asked.

Alex stood waiting at the rear of his gleaming red Mercedes with the boot lid fully extended. Jill was the first to appear followed by Jenny hauling their luggage.

"Wow.....are we going in this". Jill gasped in amazement. "Yes, this is mine, will it do ?" He joked. "Yes, it's lovely". Jill exclaimed as Axel lifted the girls bags into the boot. "Where is that brother of mine ?" "Here....just a minute". Isaac shouted from within the hotel lobby.

Jill and Jenny both received enthusiastic hugs and kisses from both of the lad's parents before they climbed into the Mercedes. Jenny in the front and Jill in the rear.

"This is a very expensive looking car Axel, is it really yours ?" Jenny cheekily enquired. "Yes it is really mine, but I must confess it was my birthday present from our parents". "Some present, I had a book from my dad". Jenny quipped. "We both had a car, I chose the Merc and Isaac chose a sporty Jaguar. His Jag is only a two door and not much room in the back. I did tell you money is not a problem. We know....we are very lucky to have generous parents". Axel concluded and proceeded to steer the car from the hotel parking area and onto the secluded narrow lanes.

"When we get back to Lauterbrunnen after the Jungfrau, we will set off straight away for Riva del Garda. It will be a long drive and we will be quite late getting to our hotel. I booked a hotel on the internet last night, I booked for three nights, so tomorrow we can have the day on the lake and on Wednesday we will go to Venice to meet your sister. It is only a couple of hours drive from Riva to

Venice". Axel said to put Jenny at ease.

"Our lot have tonight in Interlaken and then they go to Lake Maggiora tomorrow, and have a day trip to Venice from Stressa". Jill responded extending her seat belt to lean forward with her head positioned between the front seats. "I daresay we'll bump into some of them". Jenny uttered turning slightly to face her friend.

"Change of plan !" Axel suddenly announced. "We will miss Lauterbrunnen and go straight to Kleine Scheidegg and meet your party there. It will save a couple of hours by not having to wait and catch a train back to Lauterbrunnen when we finish here".

"Here they are Mave". Joe shouted with delight at seeing the girls already in conversation with Edith and Georgina. "We thought you'd changed your minds and decided not to come when you didn't get on the train at Lauterbrunnen". Mavis gushed. "Is that the lad's car ?". Joe asked, surprised to observe Axel just leaving such a prestigious gleaming red Mercedes and running to catch up with Isaac on his way to join Jill and Jenny.

"You're going to be travelling in style, is there room for me and Mave ?, We don't mind a bit of a squeeze. The coach is a dead hole without you two lasses, there's only John and Lucy left, the rest are a bunch of whatsits". Joe groaned on. "We shall miss you, look after yourselves".

"Aye up, get in line, stand easy, here

comes the lady in red with her bloody clip board". Joe added. "Red looks good on certain people, but she's definitely not one of them". Mavis chuckled as Joe watched RD's face change colour as he began singing "Lady in red".

"That glamorous woman on the other side of the platform in that tight red dress thinks you're singing to her, I should shut up Joe her husband is giving you a funny look". Mavis urged.

"You two Swiss lads can sling your hook". RD barked in her usual abrupt rude manner. Fortunately Isaac and Axel just looked at her with blank expressions and remained holding hands with their holiday girl friends waiting to get on the train for the ride through the inside of the Eiger mountain and to the top of the Jungfraujoch.

"Thank God this is the last time we'll see her till we go to the airport. I shouldn't think we'll meet her in Venice amongst all the crowds that'll be there. Mind you if she's wearing that red uniform it'll be hard not to see her". Jill uttered "What is sling your hook ?" Isaac enquired. "Oh nothing, just a daft English expression". Jill answered to avoid any reprisals from Isaac and Axel.

The train left Kleine Scheidegg station and soon entered the tunnel into the North face of the Eiger. "Have you done this before ?" Jill asked their Swiss friends. "No it is something we always wanted to do but never got round to it. It is very expensive, even using our Swiss passes". Axel retorted.

"I wouldn't know how much we've paid, ours was included in the price of the holiday". Jenny replied.

The platform at the summit was soon a mass of bodies of all nationalities and sizes as the train carriages emptied.

Jenny suddenly found herself falling and hitting the concrete platform just clear of the train. "Are you alright". Jill screeched as a small group of people formed a shield to stop other passengers pushing into her. Isaac and Axel knelt on the floor each side supporting Jenny while someone thrust a arm between the bodies to hand Jill a clean white towel to stem the blood flowing profusely from Jenny's badly grazed upper left arm.

"That wasn't an accident". Jenny snapped rubbing the scuffed knees of her jeans as she got to her feet with the help of the boys. "I was deliberately pushed, someone, and I can guess who gave me a good hard shove in my back".

"It could have been fatal if the train had started to move". Axel proclaimed. "Oh do cheer me up Axel".

"Bitte, excuse..." A lady in a uniform requested as she forced her way to be besides the invalid Jenny. The onlookers dispersed as the lady took Jenny by the hand and lead her into a small office accompanied by Jill, leaving the Swiss boys looking on through the open door.

"Sit and rest for a while my dear, you

probably just felt dizzy and lost your balance. It happens to a lot of people, feeling feint at first when you get off the train at this height". The pleasant lady official said assuming this to be the case. "No.....I did feel a bit dizzy but that wasn't the reason I fell". Jenny replied. "Someone gave me a hard shove in my back". . "That 's all nice and clean". The lady advised, choosing to ignore Jenny's statement as she proceeded to apply a bandage from Jenny's armpit to her elbow. "That should keep your arm clean until you see your doctor, please call in and see me before you go back down. Can I have your name and address ?, I need to enter the details into the accident book.

"Are you feeling alright now Jenny, do you hurt anywhere else ?" Axel asked. "You could have hit your head, you only just missed the side of the train". Isaac uttered. "Thanks Isaac, I've already just missed death from your brother trying to cheer me up". Jenny said and laughed.

"I know there was a crowd all jostling on the platform but I was deliberately pushed, and it was her". Jenny repeated. "Unless someone actually saw her do it, there's not a lot you can do, she'd only deny it". Jill advised trying to suppress Jenny's rising anger. "It's a good job we've left the coach because one of us wouldn't survive the rest of the tour, things are getting very nasty. How the hell did she get to be a tour guide, how did she get to be a human being even". Jenny snorted.

"Oh God she's over there in the queue with a couple of her cronies getting something to eat". Jenny snapped. "Let's come back in half an hour for some lunch when she's gone". Jill suggested. "No....bugger the vicious sod, you come with me Axel ?" Jenny insisted as she marched defiantly across the room and stood directly behind the massive red uniform with Axel at her side, leaving Jill and Isaac to reserve a table while watching on nervously.

"Joe and Mavis have just spotted us". Jenny uttered. "Don't ask Joe". Jenny snapped before Joe could ask, and then spent the next few minutes describing what had happened. Well almost, except for omitting that she suspected that it was RD that pushed her.

"I think we ought to think about getting going, it is half past two now, and we have a long drive to Riva". Isaac suggested

"How's your arm now Jenny ?" Jill asked. "Very sore, but it's stopped bleeding. The medical lady asked me to call in at her room to see her before we left, so I'd better pop in. You three get a seat on the train while I go and see her".

The girls realised their holiday travelling through Italy with their Swiss boyfriends in a luxurious motor car was about to begin as the train returned them to Kleine Scheidegg station.

"I didn't expect we'd have to come back to Interlaken". Jill exclaimed. "Yes I am sorry but I could not arrange for the mountains to be moved in time". Axel joked as he drove the high powered Mercedes at considerable speed but confidently along the main route towards Milan with the assurance of a much more experienced driver.

"It will be about nine o'clock by the time we get to Riva, we can stop and have a meal in Milan". Axel proposed.

After a brief stop and a hurried meal and a change of driver the red Mercedes finally drew to a halt in the hotel car park.

Four very weary travellers trudged up to the hotel reception desk. "Let us drop everything and find the lounge and have a nice cool beer or a coffee". Isaac suggested, while watching the porter load their luggage onto a trolley.

~~~~~~~~~~~~~~~~~

Day ten Tuesday

"Guten morgen". Isaac greeted, reverting to his German tongue as Jenny appeared at the open dining room door. "Did you sleep well ? How is your arm this morning ?"

"We were so tired we both went off to sleep the second we hit the pillow. I never even noticed how lovely our room is until just now. My arm must have bled a little in the night, I need a clean dressing, I must find a chemist. And I still need to buy a present for my new brother. I must get him something". Jenny replied and sat down on the remaining chair between Axel and Jill.

"Get back up Jenny, it's a buffet breakfast". Jill said. With Jill and Isaac already eating, Axel and Jenny trooped hand in hand across the floor and helped themselves to the extensive range of appetising continental style breakfast.

"How did you sleep Jill ?" Axel casually enquired as he returned from the buffet table. "It was a tiring journey yesterday but it was worth it, we can spend the whole day on the lake. Your friends will be off to Stressa this morning, do you wish you had stayed with the coach ?" Axel asked before Jill had chance to reply to his previous question. "Yes Axel I slept very well, thank you".

****

The Red Demon coach left Interlaken at nine o'clock sharp with the red demon herself assuming she now had full control of her thirty eight remaining passengers, so she thought, until Joe took up the mantel where the girls left off and decided to fight their cause.

"Someone deliberately pushed Jenny against the side of the train yesterday, did you hear about it Rose ?" he asked provocatively, creating a stir of activity from a minority of the coach travellers who hadn't known.

"Yes, I heard all about it, she wasn't badly hurt I saw her in the self service queue shortly after and she seemed fine". RD snapped revealing her resentment for the question.

"It could have been a lot worse if she'd fell onto the track, she was lucky". Joe responded trying to keep the proverbial pot boiling. "Well it wasn't....so shut up". RD snarled angrily. "So you don't know anything about it ?" Joe persisted to a point just short of accusing RD of being the perpetrator.

"Shut up Joe, you've said more than enough, you'll get yourself in trouble if you keep on. Give it a rest and let's have some peace now". Mavis urged her husband and dragged him down from his aggressive crouched standing position. "Well everyone knows she did it". He whispered to Mavis as he slumped back into his window seat location.

The whole coach was stunned into a deathly silence for the next half an hour until Dug the bug made one of his knowledgeable announcements only to be overshadowed by the red demon with her microphone suggesting her passengers take part in one of her silly games.

"You're all a set of old grumps on this tour". She said, with the intention of raising a laugh, but only managed to insult the easily offended section of the coach, causing her comment to backfire spectacularly.

And to add insult to injury she then assumed that everyone was on some sort of prescription pills. This did raise a false roar of laughter from her groupies situated at the rear of the bus.

"We'll go round the coach to see who takes the most. How many ?" She asked pointing to the couple in front pew.

"Four in the morning and three at night". The first competitor claimed. "Seven to beat". RD blasted down the microphone. The game rapidly petered out as the majority of passengers deemed it too juvenile to bother taking part, creating a hostile reaction from RD. "Bugger the lot of you". She screeched and promptly sat back on her foldaway chair and remained silent for the rest of the journey.

"This must be it, she's not going to bloody well tell us we're here. This must be our hotel". Joe uttered as he trudged down the aisle followed by Mavis and several other passengers. Joe now number one enemy of RD, held eye contact with her as he pushed past her to get from the coach.

"My God Joe, you're treading on thin ice mate, she needs someone else to go after now the girls have gone". John from Gateshead advised with caution.

"I'd imagine this is her last trip with this Demon Holidays, she's either working her notice or she's more likely to have been given the heave ho' and using the rest of this journey to get to Naples to fly home. I can't see that they would let her loose on one of their tours again". Joe responded.

"I heard the Welsh couple and one of the Toms have phoned in and reported her, so I'd say she's had the chop. I don't suppose they've got anybody to replace her for this trip. Mind you we'd be better off with nobody at all. So I'd watch out, she probably couldn't care less what she does, I think she's a bit deranged, and dangerous !" John groaned.

"Shh" Mavis butted in to prevent her husband going off on another rant. "She's going to say something".

With all thirty eight passengers now all assembled like children in a school playground, and without the microphone RD bellowed the latest instructions. "It's now half past twelve, your optional excursion on the lake to Isabella for those of you who are going starts from the jetty opposite our hotel at a quarter past two. That gives you plenty of time to settle in and get some lunch. There's plenty of nice cafes or a restaurant if you prefer. Meet me at the pier at five past". With that announcement concluded RD pushed past everyone to be first in the hotel.

"My God she's suddenly turned all proper tour guidey. She's gone all professional again". Heather, Douglas's glamorous wife whispered in Mavis's ear as the guests dragged their luggage into the hotel lobby.

"Right then Mave, grab your bag, I've got the keys, let's see if we're over these soddin' kitchens". Joe griped disdainfully.

****

"If you ask at the desk they'll probably find someone to dress your arm, they're bound to have some form of first aid". Jill proposed.

"We have just phoned and booked a day on the lake girls. The boat stops for a couple of hours at Limone, and they say there is a good market there today, so you might be able to find something for your brother". Isaac retorted on seeing Jenny re-emerge from the makeshift medical room with a crisp new white bandage to her left upper arm.

"Sorry for the breeze on the lake folks, this is normal, it occurs every day". The tall slim sun tanned youth apologised and continued. Firstly in English and then in Italian to explain the various names and reason for the differing wind strengths as the spectacle of the sail board and kite surfers flashed across the bow of the boat.

"Two hours". The handsome Italian youth shouted as he openly drooled at the sight of

Jill as she clambered from the boat wearing a pair of shrink wrap pale blue jeans and tightly fitting white cotton sweater.

"You've clicked there Jill". Jenny laughed and wandered off arm in arm with Axel in the direction of the street market, while Jill and Isaac elected to relax with a coffee at the first lakeside cafe.

"I couldn't see anything special for my brother, I ended up buying him a leather wallet and a belt. There wasn't anything else suitable for lads. I hope he likes them". Jenny moaned hopefully at the thought of giving such items as a gift to a sixteen year old boy. "I daresay he'd prefer a computer game". She added in dismay at not having made a purchase back in England.

"If you've finished with the market come and have an ice cream down by the lake before we have to get on the boat". Jill suggested.

"How do you feel about meeting your sister and your brother now it's almost here Jen, have you said where you're going to meet ?" Isaac asked. "The only place we've both heard of is Saint Marks Square, but we didn't know a specific land mark so we decided to meet right in the centre. I'm sure we'll recognise each other, we ought to, we're exactly identical, and we've arranged to be wearing the same yellow dresses. We chose them from the same catalogue a while ago, and if it happens to be raining we've each bought a see through plastic mac". Jenny replied.

"Did you enjoy your gelato girls ?" The young boat hand asked, and strolled past on his way to the pier. "Five minutes girls". He added, completely ignoring Axel and Isaac.

"Now we're going across the lake to Malcesine. You can get a nice lunch, or a ride on the cable car, or both". The lad said in his cheeky brash manner.

"That was a great day out, very interesting commentary". Axel remarked as a compliment when leaving the boat, at the same time palming a few euro coins to the tall handsome lad. Isaac wasn't as engaging when the lad made a cheeky remark to Jill as she left the boat. "He's harmless". Jill said to reassure Isaac and put her arm around his waist and waved to the boat lad as they walked away from the jetty.

"It's still only four o'clock, what are we going to do for the next two hours ?" Jill chirped as the two couples strolled with linked hands along the lake esplanade, eventually occupying a couple of benches overlooking the lake to watch the antics and acrobatics of the sail and kite surfers.

Later in the evening Jill and Isaac decided to visit a night club while Axel and Jenny stayed in the hotel lounge enjoying a glass or two of wine.

~~~~~~~~~~~~~~~~

Day eleven Wednesday

"Well you won't be needing your waterproofs Jenny, it's a beautiful day". Jill gushed, almost as excited as Jenny clomping across the Italian tiled dining room floor in her high heeled shoes.

"Last down to breakfast again Jenny". Isaac called out, inadvertently notifying the rest of the hotel guests, already captivated by the gorgeous sight of Jenny wearing a 1950's style bright yellow flowing dress hemmed just below her knees, with a tight fitting bodice. Elegantly poised on a pair of cream high heel shoes.

"My God do you want to be my girl for today". Isaac joked. "Watch it you Swiss yoghurt". Jill squeaked.

"We will call here for an hour on the way back". Axel advised as the Mercedes skirted around the town of Verona. "Our lot have an excursion to this place tomorrow on the way to Florence". Jenny replied.

Axel stared affectionately at his motor car squeezed in between other expensive looking vehicles. "It should be safe enough here. The car each side of mine is worth double what mine cost". He uttered. "Never mind how much it cost, I wished you'd look at me the way you look at your car". Jenny laughed. "Oops". Exclaimed Axel. "Anyway let's find the water bus to take us to Saint Marks

Square".

"Would you believe it, look who's over the other side of the square". Jill cried out, catching a sight of a red umbrella hovering above a glimpse of red chiffon, mostly hidden from view by the throng of tourists "What time must they have left Stressa to get here at the same time as us ?" Jenny uttered, "I assume her cronies are fluttering around that umbrella". Jenny added. "Oh well, we'll just have to make sure we avoid her. Joe and Mavis will be somewhere about, he's probably trying to catch a few pigeons". Jenny concluded with laughter.

"Why would he want to catch some pigeons, does he eat them ?" Isaac enquired seriously. "No course not you daft devil. Don't you have pigeon flyers in Switzerland ? He races them". Jill butted in. ?" "He would never win, unless he can fly ?.....Of course we have people who have pigeons". Isaac joked. "Why did I get the daft brother ?" Jill chirped.

"Not much chance of avoiding that Rose woman, she is over there with four of her friends and it looks as if she is heading this way". Isaac stated.

"Good morning you two". RD grunted with a sneer, and promptly and deliberately occupied an adjacent table. "Nice day, nice music, nice dress". She commented snidely while the small orchestra played a melody of popular tunes.

"Does she know anything about your sister ?" Axel asked. "No thank goodness, I only mentioned it to Edith and Joe, and I can't imagine either of them saying anything to anyone let alone her". Jenny muttered quietly.

"Not to worry, she's dragging her brood away, she just said something about the prices". Axel uttered and watched them dissolve into the crowded square. "Mind you, for once I agree with her, it is a little pricey in here. Let's go out of the square and find a more reasonable place". Jill demanded. "We are not worried about the cost". Isaac chirped. "We are, we're in debt to you already". Jill snapped surprising Isaac with her sharpness.

"The time has arrived Jen". Jill gushed anxiously, displaying even more excitement than Jenny. Jenny produced a heavy sigh to release her nervous tension. "Come on then Jill it's ten to one. I don't want to be late. We'll meet you lads by the water on the steps in about an hours time. You can meet my sister". Jenny said as she felt her stomach begin to churn. "Oh hang on Axel, I nearly forgot". Jenny cried and immediately unzipped Axel's back pack and removed a large brimmed straw hat, which reformed it's shape as it saw daylight. She settled the rich cream sun hat with the deep yellow band with the bow slightly to one side stylishly onto her head. Her jet black glossy shoulder length hair shining in the sunlight contrasting with the cream of the hat and the yellow of the dress.

"Oh my God Jenny you look absolutely stunning, you look like a fifties film star....... Marilyn with black hair. That fella has just took a photo of you, and now his mate's taking one. Stop posing you silly devil, you'll have everyone taking pictures in a minute. They think you're someone famous". Jill urged as another tourist flashed his camera as Jenny continued to revel in her popularity. "That's lovely. thank you girls, you look wonderful". He shouted taking a second shot of Jenny from the rear as she turned to give Axel a kiss. "Wait till you see me with my sister, she'll put a smile on you face". Jenny responded cheekily raising a whistle of approval from yet another male tourist. "You'll get arrested if you keep this up you silly sod". Jill joked.

"I can feel you trembling, you're making me nervous as well now". Jenny uttered as the two girls held hands and searched their way through the mass of tourists to the middle of the square.

"There, she's got her back to us, that lad standing beside her looks just like Axel. I can't stop shaking, that's my twin sister". Jenny murmured, with mini explosions taking place inside her chest.

"Her hair is as beautiful and the same style, onto her shoulders and jet black just like yours". Jill gasped. "Hello Diane". Jenny whispered as she was just about to turn around. Immediately the sisters wrapped their arms around each other and tears streamed across both their cheeks. Eventually they managed to kiss each other with the brims of their sun hats folding under the pressure.

After a few minutes the sisters parted

and stood a couple of feet apart holding hands just staring at each other in amazement at the likeness, as if looking at a mirrored reflection.

"I do like your outfit" Diane gushed to break the silence with tears still streaming down her face. "I like yours too". Jenny replied also fighting back the tears.

By now a small crowd of onlookers were attracted to the two girls in bright sunshine yellow dresses. Obviously realising the significance of the meeting, began to applaud and cheer and several of the men folk began pointing their cameras and mobile phones at the unaware couple.

"We must calm down Diane, is this Richard my brother ?" The tall, slim sixteen year boy looked embarrassed standing to one side carefully holding a large white cardboard box, trying to smile at a lady tourist intent on engaging the lad in conversation as to what is the occasion. Jenny held the boy's free hand and embarrassed him even further by kissing him on both cheeks, leaving his own cheeks damp with her tears.

"And this is obviously Jill, our triplet sister". Diane said and the two girls very affectionately hugged and kissed. Jenny always mentions you and I've seen lots of photos of you". Diane said enthusiastically.

"Let's get out of the limelight and find a quiet cafe to have a good old natter. There's one in the lane, we've just come from there. You must meet our fellas after". Jenny chirped. "You never said you were going on holiday with any boyfriends". Diane blurted excitedly. "We didn't, we picked them up on the way". Jill squeaked cheekily. "You mucky devils". Diane replied with a wicked smile. "We'll tell you all about them, you can meet them later, they're Swiss". Jenny added as she and Diane linked arms and joyfully skipped like a couple of six year olds. Dodging the inquisitive tourists. Jill grabbed hold of Richard's hand and followed with the lad half heartedly copying his sister while holding the white box tight against his chest.

"People are still stopping and taking our photos even here. Jill says they probably think we're some sort of celebrities". Jenny chirped. "I don't care...do you ? I'm too happy to care". Diane replied and wiped away the moisture from her cheeks.

"I don't suppose our mother is coming to see me ?" Jenny asked hopefully. "I'm sorry, mum is all self these days I'm afraid. All she's interested in at the moment is some expensive crystal chandelier on Murano. We went there on the launch from the ship. I left her there with him arranging the packing and shipping details for the damned glass trinket. It's this second husband, he totally dominates her, she has to do everything he says, it's him that insists she has nothing to do with the past. He even made mum change my name to Chambers, but I am going to change it back. He treats her like a dog most of the time, but he's loaded and she can buy what she wants" Diane realised the distress her twin sister was feeling and to comfort her she placed an arm around her shoulders.

"How is dad ?" Diane enquired softly to lighten Jenny's mood. "I always manage to get to the mail first, otherwise if he gets it, he'll hide or destroy dad's or your letters. You must get him to use the internet". Diane moaned.

"That's just wicked and cruel". Jill griped. "Well that's what he's like.....I hate him, I need a man to whisk me away. You don't happen to have a spare fella with you ?" Diane retorted.

"Richard pass me the box please. This is for you Jenny. I ordered it a while ago as soon as we'd arranged to meet. It's very delicate, it's Murano glass. I collected it this morning direct from the factory. You'll find it's a one off and I think it's very special being made in Venice where we were reunited, but it's been packed very carefully so I wouldn't attempt to unpack it until you get home. I'll give you a clue, it's inscribed 'when two sisters met' ". Diane gushed excitedly as she placed the box on Jenny's lap.

"This is for you Diane, it's not as big a box as yours, I hope you'll like it". Jenny said anxiously. "Can I open it now ?" Diane begged, and began crying all over again as she admired the gold watch. She instantly removed her own watch from her wrist. "Can I wear it now ? I'll dump this old bit of tat". She joked through her tears. "Course, put it on. Can I have your old one". Jenny pleaded, and immediately fixed it to her own bare wrist. "What happened to your arm ?" Diane asked, noticing the end of the white bandage had slipped below Jenny's dress sleeve. "That's a long story, it's all in my holiday diary, I'll send you a copy when I get home". Jenny replied and paused for a moment. "I did buy a...". She started the sentence and stopped abruptly. "Buy a what ?" Diane asked bemused. "Oh nothing I'm getting my days mixed up". Jenny excused herself.

"Richard this is for you bro". Jenny said as she felt a tear trickle from her eye as she handed him the presentation box containing the gold watch she'd bought for her father's birthday. Jill instantly looked at Jenny in disbelief.

"You can wear it now Richard, I hope you like it". Jenny said the moment he opened the box. "Thank you Jenny, I will put it on, I've never bothered with a watch before but this is fab". Jill was still looking at Jenny wondering what ever was she was thinking about.

"It's dad's birthday soon Jen. For his present I want to do an oil painting of us two meeting in Venice, Jill, will you take a photo of us down by the water holding hands like we did". Diane asked.

"Yes......I know, I've still got to try to think of a present for him". Jenny replied while reading Jill's mind and glaring at her.

"Let's drink up and go and meet these fellas of yours". Diane suggested. "Where did you meet them, are they on the coach tour with you ?" She added'

"No, we've left the coach tour, it's just the four of us touring Italy in Axel's Merc". Jenny responded and watched for Diane's reaction. "Do go on, sounds fascinating".

"We met them on a boat on a lake trip, they were amongst a wedding party, their sister was getting married. They're called Axel and Isaac, they're twins as well, not identical though, thank goodness". "Good God how many more of us are there ?" Diane said interrupting Jenny's flow. "It was all a bit like a fairy tale, they invited us to their sister's wedding at a town the other end of the lake.....I must admit, they did chat us up and charm us first, and then they asked us if we would come to the evening reception back at a hotel in Interlaken.

We had the best night of our lives, didn't we Jill ?. We told them all about our troubles on the tour". "What troubles ?" Diane again butted in. "It's all in my diary". Jenny said and continued with the story. "Anyway, they asked us to leave the coach and tour with them and they said they would get us to Naples in time for our flight home. We said no at first, Then we had another go with our rep' so we said bugger it let's do it and we did". "What was the problem with your rep' ?" Diane briefly interrupted once more. "Another long story. We stayed the first night at their parent's chalet hotel in the mountains and now we're having the rest of our holiday touring Italy with them in a luxury bright red Mercedes, and up to now it's been fantastic". Jenny gulped and paused to refill her lungs.

"How romantic, you lucky pair". Diane repeated. "I have one fella sweet on me at college, I've been out with him a few times. He's a nice bloke but a bit of a sports fanatic so when we go anywhere it's usually to a baseball or soccer match, so boring. So we'll see". Diane responded with a sigh of envy,
"As well as my paintings I have started to write short stories, I've even had one accepted by a woman's magazine. So if you will send me a copy of your diary I might be able to turn it into a story". "Definitely, I'd love to read what you can make of our holiday.....and some of the awful people on the coach". Jenny chirped.
"There is a handle on this box, didn't Richard see it ?" Jill asked as she took control of Jenny's present. "Yes we know but I told Richard to hold it close so it didn't get knocked in the crowd". Diane uttered.
"Here we are then, these are the boys. Axel and Isaac. This is my twin sister Diane and my new brother Richard". Jenny said, proudly making the introductions. "You certainly are twins, don't wander away or the wrong one might come with us". Isaac joked. "I'd already decided that". Diane ribbed and began to laugh at the thought.
Another small group had paused to gaze at the two glamorous girls, identical in looks and dress, standing at the waters edge two feet apart holding hands and looking into each other's eyes while Jill, also a good looker but with long flowing blonde hair, took several

pictures with her camera.

"Oh my God we've got an audience again, it's these dresses". Diane chirped. "There's probably a guessing game going on wondering who you are". Jill said repeating her previous comments.

"What's going on here ?" A shirt sleeved uniformed police officer enquired in English. . "You're causing an obstruction, are you filming, do you have a permit ?" He asked sharply. After a fair bit of sweet talking and flirting from the three girls he accepted their explanation and then took the girls by surprise by inviting himself on to a group photograph with all three of them to a rousing cheer from the now large gathering of curious sightseers.

"It's nearly time for me to catch the launch back to the ship, come and have a stroll with me for ten minutes Jenny". Diane requested sorrowfully. The twin sisters and Richard wandered away from the masses to find solitude on a back street canal arched bridge.

"Stay here Richard, I'll come back here to you in ten minutes". Jenny gave her brother a kiss on the cheek. "We will meet again bro". She shouted as she and Diane strolled back into the bustling Saint Marks Square.

"This is it then Diane". Jenny said softly as they reached the middle of the square. "This is where we started, I wonder whether we'll see each other again". She cried as the tears again flowed freely. "Yes we will, as soon as I've finished college I intend to apply to return to Britain to live". Diane said with determination.

Jenny returned to the quayside with streaks of mascara running down her cheeks. "Diane's gone...she says she will come back to Britain but I know she won't be able to". Jenny sobbed in Jill's arms. "Of course she will". Jill assured. "We parted in the square where we met". Jenny sniffled.

"There's a water bus waiting, shall we make our way back and we can have dinner in Verona ?" Axel suggested. "I'll carry the box now Jill, if anything gets broken it'll be my fault". Jenny urged as the two couples stood leaning on the boat rails.

"Jenny". Jill said quietly. "You see that good looking lady in the pretty coloured dress, she just gave us a sort of a wave, and now she's staring at us and smiling". Jill stated. "It can't be. It looks like her, can we get off ?" Jenny screeched. "Not now Jen we're moving". Axel retorted.

Jenny waved to the lady and the lady responded and shouted loudly. "Write to me please". And the waving continued until the water bus was out of sight.

Jenny was now even more upset, knowing her mother had turned up but didn't have the courage to defy her tyrant of a husband to make contact. She stared down at the blue waters of the Grand Canal deep in thought of what might have been, and too engrossed to notice a water ambulance creating waves in it's wake as it sped past with it's sirens blazing away.

The stop in Verona proved to be an anti-climax for Jenny, with all the excitement of meeting her sister for the first time since they were three years old, not even having any memory of Diane. And then to meet a half brother for the first time, then unable to leave the moving boat as her mother secretly waved from the quay.

"Are you not hungry Jenny?" Axel asked when the waiter reached hesitantly to remove the remains of her half eaten meal. "Would you prefer something different?" The waiter offered. "That's very kind, but no thank you". Jenny politely replied.

"You've not mentioned your arm today, is it still sore?" Jill asked. "No it hasn't hurt at all today. If it did I would never have noticed. It's almost healed, I'll think I might leave the bandage off for tomorrow". Jenny replied.

"Come on then Jen, there's some very expensive shops in this place, they'll still be open, let's go and have a browse. We'll see you two back at the car in half an hour". Jill chuntered and gave Jenny a sharp tug by the hand. "Alright but don't go buying something you can't afford". Jenny chirped in a more upbeat tone.

"Is it always going to be dark when we arrive back at our hotel?" Jill quipped. "Well I'm going straight up to bed". Jenny stated and vanished alone behind the closed lift door.

~~~~~~~~~~~~~~

Day twelve Thursday

Jenny lay awake for most of the night with her mind buzzing from the previous day, and after only a couple of hours of restless sleep she was awakened by the early dawn light creeping in the window through a parting in the curtains.

Carefully she lifted herself from the bed, then wandered across the large bedroom and quietly fully opened the curtains to let in even more daylight. Tired but unable to sleep she suddenly had an overwhelming urge to open Diane's present.

The desire to see what was in the box eventually became too much. With the room key she scored the sealing tape and opened the box lid flaps to reveal a mass of shredded packing materials. Gradually as she exposed the delicate Murano glass figurines the tears again began to stream down her face dripping like raindrops into the cardboard box.

Before she had even removed half of the packing material Jenny could see exactly what the sculpture was. With the most extreme care, and with both hands encompassing the item. Jenny lifted it clear of it's box and placed it onto a small glass top coffee table.

Jenny then climbed back into bed and lying on her side stared admiringly through her tears at the figurines and within a few minutes fell to sleep.

Come on then, you must tell us where we're going today". Jill demanded impatiently. "We did originally intend to go to Florence, but when you said your coach was going there for three nights we decided to go to the seaside instead. So we've booked a hotel on the sea front at Rimini for tonight and tomorrow we're going to Rome for a couple of nights". Isaac replied hoping for a favourable reaction.

"Oh good, me and Jenny can get to wear our new swimming costumes, none of the hotels have had a swimming pool". Jill happily responded. "Oh great, something for me and Axel to look forward to". Isaac added cheekily.

"Here she comes, last again, good job the breakfasts are always a cold buffet". Isaac called out, and again alerting the other diners to Jenny as she weaved between the tables.

"What did you all think about my present from Diane ?" Jenny asked. "Absolutely fantastic". Jill gushed. "She must have sent a photo of herself to the company wearing the yellow dress and the hat, and the shoes. It's so beautiful, it's even got your faces and the pose of the two figurines exactly as you and Diane faced each other holding hands when you met".

"Are we all ready ?. I have repacked your figures, yes.......don't ask they are perfectly safe. I packed the box as before. It's safe in with the luggage". Axel said. "The seaside here we come". Isaac chirped like an excited ten year old going on an annual holiday. "Jill told me they have bought new swimming costumes especially for us". Isaac joked. "Cheeky sod, you'll be too busy making sand castles with your buckets and spades to keep up with us mature women when we hit the beach". Jill quipped making Jenny laugh for the first time since Venice.

"We can thank Jenny for the early start, so let's make the best of it". Axel uttered and drove the Mercedes out of the hotel car park and along the lake esplanade.

"We were going to stop for a bite to eat at Modena, but you were fast asleep Jenny. That was probably because you were up half the night opening your present. Did you eventually get some sleep ?" Isaac asked.

The satnav informed of the destination arrival and Axel parked his vehicle within the yellow parallel lines immediately in front of the beachside hotel. "Right then ladies.....lunch, beach and bikinis....we are here". Isaac jested.

"I'm not keen on the look of that lot, there's millions of chairs and rows of umbrellas". Jill groaned in dismay. "It will be alright, I asked at the desk about it, They told me to go to a certain sector and that the water front loungers cost a bit more, so I got the receptionist to reserve one with four loungers. I was going to suggest we stayed another night, but seeing this we will leave it as it is". Axel responded.

"This isn't too bad". Jill said as they

reached their front row waterside positions. Jill and Jenny immediately slipped out of their beach robes and slowly walked on the hot sand to the water's edge standing looking at the blue sea with the sun in their faces.

"Wow...Isaac purred, as he and Axel watched the girls walk the short distance to the water and stared with admiration at their figures silhouetted by the midday sun.

After the long morning drive and the exhausting heat of the afternoon spent on the beach, followed by dinner and a one am finish in a crowded night club, the four companions decided to call it a night.

~~~~~~~~~~~~~~~

Day thirteen Friday

"Rimini might not be your favourite place but today's drive is nearly all along the coast according to the satnav route. Come on Jill". Axel shouted to hurry her along as the three of them sat in the heat of the purring Mercedes. "Is this going to be one of those scary cliff edge rides?" Jenny asked. "This is a big car for someone your age, how long have you been driving?" Jenny probed. "Me and Isaac both past our tests first time, shortly after our eighteenth birthday, and our parents bought us a car each for our birthday. We've drove you this far without any problems. We've been driving round the farm since we were twelve, so we do know what we're doing". Axel replied reassuringly.

****

The chatter on the coach leaving Stressa was beginning to overheat and getting very fraught with regard to an assault that had occurred during their excursion to Venice the previous day. The news filtering through the vehicle that a couple in the party, Harold and Sonia, had been near the crime scene shortly after it had happened and had watched the victim being carried to the water ambulance on a stretcher.

Mavis and Joe and several other of the

passengers stood in the aisle and moved as close as possible to the couple and strained to listen to their account of the event.

"We saw the two girls with their boys earlier in the morning having a coffee on the terrace in Saint Marks Square, and the one girl, I never knew which was which, was wearing a yellow dress exactly like the girl who'd been stabbed, and from where we were standing in the square it certainly looked like her. I think it was the girl Jenny". The husband of the couple described what he and his wife had seen to those listening.

The news was quickly relayed throughout the coach. "The lad who went on the water ambulance with her looked very much like one of the Swiss fellas they've gone off with". He added.

"Hold on Mave, we don't know if it was Jenny, it could be anybody wearing a yellow dress". Joe said comforting his wife as the tears trickled down her face. "How do you know the girl was stabbed ? She might not be too badly hurt". Joe called out from his position several pews away.

"It looked pretty bad, the ambulance crew worked on her for ages, she looked unconscious and had tubes everywhere when they finally got her to the ambulance. There was lots of blood all over her dress. The police shifted us all out of the square and roped it off".. He said breathlessly.

""Did anyone watch a news on tele this morning ?" Ex steelworker John shouted down the coach. "I had the tele on but I didn't take much notice, it looked like a news programme but it was all in Italian". The younger of the two Toms called back. John glanced across the aisle at Joe with a look of exasperation on his face. "Stupid boy". He whispered in a Captain Mainwaring voice.

"How about the driver. Have you seen the news this morning Giovanni ?" John again shouted but in the opposite direction.

"No he hasn't, and he's concentrating on the driving". RD blasted over her microphone. "You're quiet this morning Rose, did you see the girls in Venice yesterday ?" Joe asked sinisterly. "No I didn't". "Yes you did Rose, you was with me and Sylvia and Stan and Barbara, we sat next to them by the band playing in the square". "Oh yes, I remember, I probably wasn't interested enough to even notice them". RD snapped. "You actually commented on the one girls dress". "Did I ? I don't remember". RD said abruptly and looking very annoyed at one of her supposed friends and then immediately began to make an announcement to deflect the unwanted questions.

"She bloody did it". Joe whispered to John across the aisle. "Shh Joe, Be careful, she'll hear you. You can't go round saying things like that". John cautioned. "She bloody did it". Joe repeated.

"Did anybody else see the girls in Venice yesterday ?" Joe shouted both ways as he again left his seat to stand in the aisle.

"The driver asked you all to remain in your seats and stop wandering around the coach. He said to keep your seat belts fastened". RD willingly bellowed hoping to kill off the conversation and the searching questions.

Joe reluctantly ignored Giovanni's request and again wandered down the central aisle. Sitting almost at the rear of the coach, Edith with her sister had little chance to contribute to the conversation. Edith fearful of standing, and even more so walking around on the moving vehicle.

"Edith". Joe chirped. "Did the girls tell you anything about going to Venice with the Swiss lads ?" "Yes, I wanted to say something earlier but I don't feel safe without my seat belt on. Yes, she was going to meet her twin sister she hadn't seen since they were three .years old. She said that was the only reason they booked this holiday because it was the only tour that had an excursion to Venice on the same day as the cruise ship her sister was on would be there. The ladies watch she bought was a present for her, the other was for her dad".

"You don't happen to have either of the girls phone numbers by any chance ?" Joe asked hopefully. "No.....I wonder where they are, I do hope it wasn't Jenny". Edith murmured.

"Jenny told me and Mavis the same about meeting her sister, did she ever say whether they were identical or not". Joe asked

Edith while wearing his Helical Spirol hat. "No........... strange, you'd have thought if they were identical she would have said....Just a thought". Joe proffered and returned to his seat with the sound of RD's rasping condemnation via her microphone ringing in his ears. "I'll ram that bloody mic' down her throat before this holiday's over". Joe snarled and shuffled into his seat beside his wife.

The noisy cross seated chattering and speculating as to whether the girl was in fact Jenny continued throughout the journey.

"What's she going to say now ?" John whispered to Joe, seated the other side of the aisle seeing the red demon get to her feet and turn to face the rear of the coach with her bright red lips pressed hard against the head of the microphone.

"We'll shortly be stopping at Medena to allow you to get some lunch. I can't tell you anything about this place. I've never been here before. We'll stop for a couple of hours, so you have plenty time to find somewhere to eat and do a bit of shopping or sight seeing".

"No change there then, she's never known anything about any of the places we've been to. You'd think she'd pretend and at least take an interest and look up some details". Joe said out loud enough to be heard either end of the coach.

"Back on the coach at half past two, and we should be in Florence by four". She bellowed as if in need to warn the local residents.

"Would you and Georgina like to tag along with us four?" Joe asked and cheekily John linked arms with Georgina and Joe with Edith. Mavis and Lucy smiled at each other in approval of the kindness shown by their menfolk.

****

"What on earth made you give your dad's present to Richard, You do realise you gave him a fifteen hundred pound watch?" Jill asked. "I know....it was a bit silly, but I couldn't see him wanting a belt and a wallet, and I had nothing else. So I had to give him something". Jenny griped. "So your dad gets a belt and a wallet then". Jill quipped.

"I've still got a couple of weeks. It won't be an expensive watch though, I'll have to stick something on my credit card. Isaac, I've bought you a wallet. Axel, I've bought you a belt, real leather". Jenny said with a giggle.

The conversation continued as the Mercedes approached their lunch stop. "Your parents called you Axel, so why didn't they call Isaac Alex, that would have been the clever thing to do". Jill asked in jest. "They did intend to but I told them there and then that I did not want to be an anagram of him". Isaac replied. "Oh God he's gradually convincing me that I really have got the daftest brother". Jill said repeating her earlier fond observation.

We'll stop here and get something to eat, it's about half way to Rome". Axel advised.

"It's the end of the coast road, we're going to leave the sea views now. We have about another two hour drive and it's only just half past twelve". Axel added and slowly toured the side streets of Toramo-Mare searching for a suitable restaurant.

"That was a lovely ride along the coast, pity the roof wouldn't come off". Jill said, sitting holding hands with Isaac in the rear seat. "You yawning again Jenny, it must be all that fresh air, or something......opening presents in the middle of the night". Isaac chirped as she stifled another yawn.

Just as Axel had predicted, another two hour drive brought the not so shiny, slightly dusty red Mercedes into the centre of Rome and to their hotel just a few hundred yards from the Colosseum.

With the knowledge that after two solid weeks of wall to wall sunshine the weather was forecast to change for the worse, so the four happy wanderers immediately hired a couple of Lambretta motor scooters and with Axel and Isaac in control set off in the mid afternoon sun to tour the city. "Well if I'm Bobby Darin then Jill's Sandra Dee, you must be Rock Hudson and Jenny is Gina Lollobrigida. I saw this film, Come September, at our village hall the other day". Isaac commented. "Thank goodness you didn't see Quadrophenia". Jill responded.

~~~~~~~~~~~~~~~~

Day fourteen Saturday

"Just in case you're wondering Mave, the Baggies are at home to Southampton this afternoon, we should beat them". Joe chirped. "Oh good". Mavis replied sarcastically almost choking on her cornflakes. "Never mind your stupid football, I want to know where Jill and Jenny are". "Well if they're in Florence they're going to get wet, it's absolutely tipping it down". Joe answered. "How can we find out if it was Jenny who was stabbed ?" Mavis urged. "We don't really know if it was a stabbing, the only way we can find out is the news or a paper, that's if they've released the girls name. It's a pity we're not on the coach today and ask Giovanni if he knows anything". Joe griped. "And there's no point buying a paper. We could get an English newspaper, it might be in there, especially if it involves an English person. I'll pop out in a minute and find one, it'll probably be yesterdays". Joe added.

"Morning you two, mind if we join you ?" Lucy asked and promptly sat next to Mavis. "John still in bed ?" Joe joked. "He's gone straight to the buffet......here he is".

"I picked this up late last night off a chair in the lounge". John said referring to the Italian newspaper he placed on the corner of the table.

"I can't read any of it but this item is definitely about the stabbing in Venice". John retorted with the paper already folded to reveal the article concerned. "I would have knocked on your door but it had gone twelve when I came upstairs. All I can make out is the girls name, Diane Chambers and another name Richard Chambers". John uttered.

"That could be Jenny's sister then, so Jenny must be okay, thank goodness. Her poor sister though. I wonder whether Jenny knows". Mavis cried.

"Was there anyone on reception when you just came through ?" Joe asked. With his mouth too full of food to verbally reply John nodded. "Back in a minute". Joe chuntered as he whipped the paper from the table.

"Yes that is the name of the girl who was stabbed and the lad named Richard is her brother. It says the brother had informed the police that she had just left her twin sister after meeting her for the first time since they were three. He says that they were just on their way back to catch the launch to return to their cruise ship. He said the two sisters looked and were dressed identical. Several other witnesses had come forward and said they'd seen the two girls together shortly before the assault. It stated that her stepfather was still on board the ship, but they didn't know the whereabouts of her mother. The fella at the desk read it out to me". Joe recited almost word for word.

"I know she did it, she thought it was Jenny, the bugger ! Where is she anyway, she's keeping out of the way". Joe snarled.

"Don't say we know anything, let her think she murdered Jenny, she'll have a big surprise when the girls come back to the coach. That's if she hasn't found out for herself or been arrested by then. Be as well because I think Jenny would throttle her when she sees her". Joe added with his temper beginning to get the better of him.

"What about Edith ?" Lucy asked. "Yes tell Edith, but tell her to keep it to herself, not to tell anyone else at all". Joe replied and dispensed with his detective's hat for the rest of the day.

"Well there isn't anything we can do, so how are we going to pass the time. I'd love to look around Florence but it's wet and blowing a gale at the moment". Mavis moaned

"Edith came wandering aimlessly into the dining room looking distressed and lost. "Edith". John shouted, intending to tell her the news about Jenny. But before he had chance to speak Edith began to quietly cry. "Georgina's gone missing again". She blurted out loud. "I only went to the bathroom for five minutes and she'd gone. I was sure she'd be down here, you haven't seen her ? Oh God where is she". "Sit down, we'll have a look, we'll find her, she can't have gone far". John said sympathetically. "What if she's gone outside in this weather, she was only wearing a summer dress when I went into the bathroom". "She'll still be in the hotel somewhere". Mavis said in an attempt to calm her fears.

Joe and John rushed out into the street

in just their flannels and short sleeved shirts, while the ladies searched the corridors and peeked into all the empty and open bedroom doors. Seeing Edith upset, Douglas's wife, Heather moved over and sat beside her and tried to console her.

"What's up with Edith ?" A gruff sounding woman enquired as she passed by carrying her plate of food. "Georgina's gone missing". Heather explained.

"Not again, I said she was ridiculous bringing someone with dementia on a coach tour. She's ruining everyone else's holiday". She added harshly. "Oh do go away you evil woman. I think our rep' and your like have already done that". Heather responded quietly and in her usual dignified manner.

Joe came running back into the hotel and standing impatiently at the desk in his own private pool of water, shouted for the desk clerk to call him a taxi urgently.

"Have you seen her Joe ?" John gasped exhausted as he also stood in the water that drained from his clothes.

"She got on a soddin' bus and it left before I could get across the road. I took the bus number. I've just asked this fella and he's trying to order me a taxi. A cab driver should know where that number bus goes. I've just explained to this chap what's happened". Joe uttered, indicating the male hotel receptionist with a movement of his eyes.

The desk receptionist finished the hurried conversation. "Come with me sir, I know that bus route. Someone is bringing a car round for us". "Stay here John and tell the women". Joe instructed as he followed the hotel clerk back out into the rain sodden street and the waiting vehicle. "Let's hope she stays on the bus, keep your eyes open at the stops". He ordered.

"That should be your bus". The hotel driver uttered as he pulled in behind and allowed the stationary single decked vehicle to move away from the bus stop. "If she hasn't already got off, she must still be on the bus". Joe deduced. "All we can do is to stay behind the bus and check every stop, she'll eventually have to get off at the terminus". The driver said, also stating the obvious.

As the bus came to it's resting point at the terminus, Joe jumped from the hotel car and ran to the bus exit door. "You can't get on here sir". A tall stout uniformed corporation bus employee shouted as the few remaining passengers trying to leave the bus were having to avoid Joe as he partially blocked their path, anxiously trying to look inside the bus.

"What are you doing on here Georgina ?" Joe gushed with relief at seeing the lonely elderly bedraggled lady sitting half way down the bus. The hotel receptionist explained the situation to the driver who was insisting on payment for her fare, and at the same time he threw his jacket to Joe.

Joe pulled a few euro coins from his trouser pocket and annoyingly dropped them into the driver's hand showing his exasperation at the driver's intolerance, and then proceeded to wrap the coat around Georgina's soaking wet fragile frame and supported her as he walked her to the warmth of the car.

A small crowd had gathered at the hotel entrance waiting for the return of the hotel vehicle. "They've found her". Edith screeched, and as the car stopped at the kerbside she let go of Heather's hand and rushed to open the car rear door. John and Joe assisted Georgina safely back to her room with Edith anxiously hovering, urgently wanting to get her elder sister out of her wet clothes. "Thank you". She gushed gratefully as she ushered the two men from the bedroom.

"She'll be alright, no harm done, just a bit wet". Joe said making light of his contribution in bringing Georgina back safely. Mavis looked at her husband with admiration and murmured. "People think you're a bit of a rogue and a rough diamond but you're a great bloke at heart". "Oh shut up Mave, I'm just going up stairs to get changed from these wet clothes". Joe chuntered still wiping water from his face as it constantly dripped from his mass of greying unruly hair.

"What are we going to do in this weather Joe ?". Mavis moaned. "Well me and John are going to get dried out and sit in the lounge with a pint for starters". Joe replied.

****

A few miles away in the wet and windy capital, Jill, Jenny and the Swiss lads were also sitting down to breakfast.

"That makes a change, it's Jill's turn to be last down this morning. Isaac only just beat you". Axel chirped. "Any ideas what to do today ? It's a howling gale out there". Jenny griped. "We've still got the scooters". Isaac said. "You can stick that thought, I'm not getting on the back of scooter and whipping around Rome in this". Jill replied. I think I'd sooner go back to bed". The boys resisted the temptation to respond.

"Well at least they've got an indoor pool in this hotel, it's down in the basement. We can have a swim first, it'll pass the morning away. It's a nice pool with loungers and a bar". Axel remarked. "So let's see you in those fantastic costumes again". He added with a cheeky grin.

"This weather is forecast to be around for several days, shall I see if I can book on a sight seeing tour bus for this afternoon ? At least we'll be in the dry. And we must be able to find a decent night club for the evening. And we can always have another couple of hours by the pool". Isaac suggested.

~~~~~~~~~~~~~~~~~

Day fifteen Sunday

On the last full day before the girls rejoin the coach, they and their Swiss boyfriends prepare for a three hour drive from Rome to Sorrento for their last overnight stay, while RD and her coach party visit Formia, a seaside town a couple of hours away from Sorrento for their final night.

"Jenny wins the prize for being last down this morning". Isaac chuckled cheekily. Jenny stormed across the dining room and stood, seething with anger, firmly gripping hold of the back of Axel's chair for support.

"Who's rattled your cage this morning, had a bad night ?" Jill joked. Jenny refrained from rising to Jill's remark.

"Diane was stabbed in the back in Venice just after we'd said goodbye". Jenny blurted out, causing other diners close by to take an interest. Before Jill or the lads had chance to respond to her blunt statement, Jenny screeched hysterically. "It was that bloody woman, I know it, she probably thought it was me. I'll bloody kill her". "Is Diane going to be alright, she's not dead, is she ?" Jill cried. "No, she's alive, just". Jenny snapped.

"How do you know all this ?" Axel asked. "They think she's going to pull through, she's in hospital in Milan. Richard my half brother just phoned me that's why I'm late coming down.

He looked in Diane's phone but he couldn't get through on the number so he tried to ring dad in Swindon, but dad's been away. He must have come back home yesterday. He said he finally spoke and told him about Diane just before he rang me. Dad gave him my new number, I'd just changed it because of the horrible calls I'd been getting".

"I'm going to find out where the coach park is". Jenny snarled and immediately began to leave the dining room. "Where are you going, we have got all day to do that. Come back and have some breakfast". Axel pleaded.

"She might have already been arrested". Isaac offered to ease Jenny's stress. "She might have, if anybody saw her do it. I wonder whether they know anything about it on the coach". Jenny responded.

The remainder of morning spent in Sorrento turned into one of misery for Jenny and the others as they wandered round the town on foot in the pouring rain and blustery conditions. Finally they located the coach park.

With nothing in the way of entertainment apparently available indoors the local cafes seemed the only option to shelter from the weather. Isaac's jocular suggestion to hire a couple of scooters again didn't get the reception he expected.

After about an hour and a few coffees followed by an early lunch, with some information from the proprietor, Jill and Isaac settled for an afternoon at one of the town cinemas.

"I don't fancy an afternoon staring at a foreign film....no not even on the back row". She chirped before Axel could make one of his usual quips. "We could go for a ride on the bus to keep dry. Let's go on the Amalfi Drive, we needn't get off the bus, we can stay on the bus and come straight back". Jenny proposed. "We might as well spend an hour in Amalfi, we could have a coffee". Axel suggested. "Not more coffee". Jenny groaned.

~~~~~~~~~~~~~~~~~~

Day sixteen Monday

"No, you and Axel get going, you've got a heck of a drive today if you intend to reach Milan in one go". Jenny insisted in reply to the Swiss lads offer to escort Jenny and Jill to the coach to give her support when she confronts her enemy.

"Well make sure you give me a ring as soon as you can, to let me know how you got on". Axel demanded.

After a passionate farewell the girls stood in the driving rain with the wind in their faces, their cheeks becoming red raw and wet with a mixture of tears and rainwater.

"We will keep in touch and we will see you again, probably sooner than you think". Isaac shouted as Jenny and Jill waved sorrowfully and watched Axel slowly drive the red Mercedes from the hotel car park.

"I hope so, but as soon as they get back home they'll forget all about us". Jill said.

"Oh well Jill, let's hope it's not the end. Anyway let's go and get our things packed, the coach will be there in half an hour".Jenny sighed

****

"I'm glad we found out that it wasn't Jenny who'd been stabbed or we'd be worried that Jill was going to turn up on her own". Joe whispered to avoid RD or anyone else hearing. RD had now taken up residence a couple of yards along the aisle from Joe and Mavis, occupying the more comfortable double seat vacated by the girls.

Poor Edith was teetering around the edge of her nerves in case her sister decided to have a bad day. "How are you this morning Georgie". Lucy asked in an effort to include her in the conversation. "She seems fine this morning". "I can speak for myself, yes I am feeling very well". Georgina interrupted.

"If you ask her she won't have remembered a thing about yesterday". Edith said quietly as her sister stared vacantly at the water racing down the outside face of the coach windows.

"She's kept her self to herself for the last few days, she's hardly spoke a word". Joe whispered again as RD walked to the front of the coach. "Shh, Joe she's going to say something". Mavis urged.

For once without the help of the microphone, which she never was really in need, RD made a brief announcement. "We're going to be in Sorrento in a few minutes and we are a lot earlier than expected, so we have plenty of time to kill". "That's an appropriate word from her". Joe shouted out, unable to resist the temptation, although it did come out slightly louder than he intended.

RD scowled and without offering any rebuke, turned her back and sat on her perch next to the driver.

For the third consecutive and final day of the tour the weather was absolutely atrocious. The gale force wind could be felt buffeting the coach as it approached it's penultimate stop.

"Here we are then, ladies, gentlemen and any other sorts". RD muttered with her voice cracking slightly as if she was either feeling emotional at leaving her passengers, which is most unlikely, or more to the point, feeling nervous at the thought of seeing Jill without her friend.

On this final day RD chose to dress casually, presumably because she would be heading home or off to find new employment.

The moment the bus stopped RD shouted. "Be back by four". And jumped from the bus with her yellow bag in her hand.

"Where's she going". Dug the bug asked as he watched her marching away and disappear down a lane.

"Grab you bags Jill, let's go". Jenny shouted with her heart beginning to pound at the thought of confronting her nemesis. The girls found the ten minute estimated walk turned into twenty five minutes as they battled against the ferocious wind with their wheeled luggage drifting sideways with each gust. Jenny also had to contend with the large cardboard box containing her delicate glass figurines, especially with the outside of the box getting damp and showing signs of immanent collapse.

Joe spotted Jill and Jenny approaching

the coach from his window seat and in an instant physically forced Mavis to stand and squeezed past to get into the aisle. "What the hell are you playing at Joe, you trod on my foot you big lumux". She cursed.

"Jill and Jenny, they're here". He gasped like a long lost husband returning from a war zone, as he pushed past several fellow passengers standing to put on their wet weather coats.

"Hiya girls". Joe gushed with the hope of a greeting kiss. But before he had chance to elaborate Jenny stormed past him and climbed onto the coach.

"Where is the bitch ?" Jenny screeched, looking up and down the bus with no regard to the height, size and weight disadvantage she possessed.

"She's not here Jenny, you've just missed her, she went about twenty minutes ago". Mavis said in a calm voice as she attempted to squeeze down the aisle. "It's probably just as well, the mood you're in Jenny. I think if she was here you'd want to kill her". Jill snapped. "You're right...I bloody well would". Jenny shrieked hysterically. "Anybody know where the evil bugger went ?" Jenny raged.

"Here, come and sit down for a minute and calm down". Jill insisted. "We heard all about your sister Jenny, I'm sure she'll be alright". Mavis said passionately. "I hope so, she's still in an induced coma, but I phoned the hospital just before we left our hotel this morning and they say she's out of danger". Jenny replied. "They say they're hoping to fly her back to America in a couple of weeks time, so things are looking better. My mum is with her now. I thought I saw her in Venice just as we were leaving, she must have missed the same launch that Diane and Richard should have caught. At least she's behaving like a mother should. Her husband is still on the cruise apparently. I'll still kill that bitch when she comes back". Jenny cried repeating her threat..

"Why on earth would RD want to harm your twin sister for goodness sake ?" Came the feeble voice of her most ardent supporter. "Someone explain to the silly woman...Because she thought it was Jenny". Jill snapped displaying her annoyance. "She still thinks it was you as far as we know". Jill added.

"You never said what Richard told you about Diane getting stabbed". Jill mooted. "I was too upset at the time. He said he was in front of Diane weaving a way through the crowds when Diane just let out a shriek and stopped and put her hand on her back and it was covered in blood and then she dropped onto her knees and slowly fell to the ground on her face. A man and his wife tried to stop the bleeding by pressing their hands on her back. And someone else put a coat under her head. Richard thought she was dead".

"That must have been where that water ambulance was going that past us on the ferry". Jill uttered.

"Apart from this terrible upset how was your holiday with your Swiss boys ?" Mavis asked with tongue in cheek in the hope of lifting Jenny's spirits.

"They set off from our hotel about an hour ago, they wanted to stop and see us okay, but we persuaded them to get going, they've got a whole days drive to Milan. We stayed here in Sorrento last night". Jill explained. "And did you have a good time ? Any hope of a fairy tale romance, are you going to see them again or is that it ?" Mavis asked excitedly.

"We were having a fantastic time up until yesterday morning when Richard phoned me. We knew nothing about it......Yes we are going to see them again, so they said, and yes it was very romantic. I've fallen for Isaac and I know Jenny is head over heels for Axel, but we'll have to see". Jill said sincerely then listed all the places they'd visited and the things they'd done.

"And what about the coach tour, did it get any better after we left ?" Jill asked. "You must be joking, Joe actually accused the red demon of pushing you off the platform up at the Jungfrau". Mavis responded,

"He's missed you two girls. Look at the daft devil, he loves the both of you as if you were his daughters". Mavis chirped. "And we love him, and you Mavis, you were the only couple who stood by us at first". Jenny piped in, now in a less aggressive frame of mind.

"Anyway what do we do now, it's

horrible weather and I don't fancy sitting on this coach for the next four hours". Joe griped and reached his all weather anorak from the overhead shelf.

"Did your sister like the present you bought her ?" Edith asked politely. "Yes she loved it, she put it on right away, I'm wearing her old one". Jenny said holding up her left arm. "I wish I could show you what she gave me, it's a Murano glass figurine of me and Diane posing exactly how when we met. It's beautiful, but it's very delicate and I'm frightened to try and unpack it again". Jenny added and gently pushed the box along onto the window seat. "Ask her what she gave her brother". Jill uttered. "Alright I know how stupid it was but you needn't tell anyone. I couldn't find anything suitable....I gave him dad's watch". Jenny responded and gave Jill a disapproving stare. Edith decided not to enquire further for fear of causing the two friends to fall out.

"I suggest we pop in and out of the shops to start with, that'll pass an hour away".. Lucy, Tynesider John's lady friend said interrupting the group. "What do you want to do John, do you think there's a snooker hall handy ?" Joe joked.

"Well come on then, let's go and brave the weather and wander round these shops". John uttered.

"Surely the shops are open ?" Lucy enquired hopefully. "Only the odd one or two are open, what shall we do ?" Lucy lamented at her unfortunate suggestion. "If we were closer we'd have time to go to Pompeii, you know, the town that was buried when the volcano erupted in......a long while ago". John replied, the date of the eruption eluding him..

"Come on, let's get on that bus for the Amalfi Drive, we can get off at Positano and at least spend a couple of hours having a pizza down by the sea". Joe suggested as he began to jostle his way on to the bus dragging his wife by her arm, leaving the others no option but to follow his lead. "Just get on the bus, you get bugger-all for being polite here". Joe shouted coarsely.

"Me and Mavis came on the Amalfi Drive and went to Positano a few years ago when we had a holiday in Sorrento for our fortieth anniversary". Joe uttered. "We came on it yesterday". Jenny chuntered. "Me and Axel went down to Amalfi for the afternoon".

"They only put learners on this route, it's supposed to be too dangerous to risk losing their good drivers". Joe said in an attempt at a joke as the bus veered from side to side with each strong gust of wind.

"The driver could have heard you say that, your mouth will get you in trouble one of these days". Mavis murmured.

"Where do you reckon RD's gone off to". "Joe quipped. "The last bulletin she gave she said she'd be with us until the airport. She said she was going to work her way back to Switzerland in time for the winter season". John answered. "She reckons she's an experienced skier, if you can believe her. I'd give my Albion season ticket to a Wolves fan to see her flying over a mountain cliff edge". Joe snapped.

"I don't think she does any skiing, I heard her telling her mates that she takes charge of a ski chalet and looks after six or eight people at a time". Lucy said contributing to the conversation. "God help the poor devils". Mavis replied.

The bus came to a juddering halt as if the driver had just been given instructions to perform an emergency stop. "My God, this wind's powerful".John gasped on leaving the warmth of the bus, with one hand holding his flat cap on his head and the other trying to keep his plastic raincoat from taking off.

Once inside the comparative shelter of the narrow lanes they zig zagged down the steep slopes to the beach.

"Oh my goodness, it's impossible to stand against this wind". Mavis moaned while the six silly English holiday makers were almost leaning at forty five degrees into the wind in defiance of it's strength.

After a few foolish minutes of bracing themselves against the hurricane force conditions and suffering the fierce sea spray and facial stinging from being whipped with black sharp volcanic ash from the shore, they made a dash for the beach side restaurant.

Apart from one other couple the restaurant seemed empty, until Jenny spotted a familiar giant of womanhood sitting alone in a far corner. "No..Jill shouted, and hung on tightly to her friend's arm. "Surprised to see me, you murderer", Jenny screamed. "Stop it Jen, be sensible, if she did it the law will deal with her. You'll only get yourself in trouble if you do something silly". Jill insisted and pulled Jenny down into her chair. "Just ignore her and let's have some lunch". Mavis interjected.

"What a load of miserable creeps they are on this tour, we've never had a coach holiday with such a bunch of obnoxious sods. And then there's that object over in the corner. You two girls added some fun, and glamour into the holiday for us. After you'd gone we were only left with Heather". Joe said loud enough to be heard anywhere in the restaurant, and concluded with a cheeky wink at Jill and Jenny. "You're asking for a good smack, me and Lucy will sort you out later, you cheeky pig". Mavis quipped.

"Rose is getting up to go, she's left all her meal". Lucy said as RD had to pass close to their table to leave the restaurant.

"Are you happy to see me still alive". Jenny snarled sarcastically. "I don't know what you're on about". "The stabbing in Venice, that's what I'm on about". Jenny snarled. "I know nothing about any stabbing, I felt ill and went back to sit in our coach after I saw you with your Swiss lads". Rose snapped back. "You're a liar. I know it was you". Jenny barked and threatened aggression towards this woman totally dismissing the advantage in RD's favour.

"I'll see you back at the coach, don't be

late or we'll go without you". Rose said casually trying to ignore Jenny's unwise threat.

The moment RD went from view Jenny became edgy and showing signs of increased anger. Eventually unable to hold her temper she jumped from her chair taking the others by surprise and ran from the restaurant.

"Stop, Jen". Jill screamed. "Wait I'll come with you". She screamed again. Jenny waited just outside and realising she wasn't dressed for the weather conditions, stepped back inside the restaurant with Jill to put their waterproof clothing back on. "Don't go and do anything foolish Jenny", Mavis shouted.

RD was gasping breathlessly and already standing with a couple of English tourists as she waited at the bus stop on the opposite side of the road when the girls reached the top of the steps.

Jenny gained control of her temper and for a few minutes she and Jill chatted with the man and woman. "You've just missed a bus, we got off it, we've come up from Amalfi. Is it worth going down to the bottom ? Is there anywhere to get out of this atrocious weather?" The man asked holding his lapels tightly to his neck. "There's a couple of decent restaurants but the place is a bit deserted and very windy". Jill replied.

The wind and the rain soon claimed victory and the couple made a dash across the road to the calmer shelter of the steep alleyways and stopped for a couple of minutes to readjust their clothing.

"Come on Jenny, we've still got a few hours before our coach leaves, and there's no saying when the next bus will be along so lets start walking back to Sorrento. It's got to be better than waiting here in this weather and with her for company". Jill proposed in an attempt to part the warring pair.

Within the first few yards of their walk, Jill's plastic rain hat was blown from her head and took off like a kite and disappeared over the stone wall and out of site.

Jenny looked back to see RD laughing at Jill running in vain after her hat. "I can see it, it's caught up on some brambles". Jill shouted loud in order to be heard above the sound of the relentless wind.

"There's a bus coming". Jill shouted in just enough time for the girls to run back about twenty yards to the stop that they had just passed after struggling to walk against the wind for about an hour.

"Look who's on here". Jill exclaimed. "You couldn't have stayed on much longer that us". She added as they sat in the pair of seats immediately in front of Joe and Mavis.

"We stayed quite awhile after you left, we all had a pudding and another pot of tea". Mavis said. "Only one other couple came into the restaurant". She added. "That would be the English couple we were chatting to at the bus stop". Jenny responded.

"Where did RD get to, she's not on the bus ? Jenny was getting a bit aggressive with RD so I persuaded her that we could walk back, otherwise I think Jenny might have come off worse". Jill said to Jenny's obvious refusal to have accepted the inevitable. "It was hard work and damn dangerous, with no footpaths". Jill spouted.

"I bet you're glad of the bus, you both look as if you've gone ten rounds with Tommy Cooper". Joe chirped. "I think you mean Henry, Joe". John called out from across the aisle.

"It feels like we've got another ten year old at the wheel". Joe joked as every gust of wind tried to push the bus sideways. "I think we'll go back and sit in the coach for the next hour or so. Did you see the size of those waves down there Joe ?". John said. "If we'd thought to bring our boards with us we could have done a bit of surfing". Joe made the daft reply in his strong Midland accent. "There's one good thing about Joe's accent". Mavis retorted and added. "He can insult who the hell he likes, even if they understand English, they'll never know what my husband said".

"Oh Gorrd, another emergency stop". Joe quipped as the bus came to a shuddering halt. "Was anyone actually driving that bus ?" A well rounded gentleman remarked in a broad American drawl as he breathlessly tried to keep pace with the girls and went to the much larger bus parked alongside the yellow coach emblazoned with red demons. John and Lucy led the following stampede across the coach park to the shelter of the bus. John with his ram rod posture, marching as if leading a platoon of marines with Lucy struggling along behind.

"That's better". Mavis gushed, now settled in the window seat with a fresh down pour of rain bouncing off the glass panels. "Only just in time, it's started to tip it down again". Douglas called out climbing onto the bus followed by his glamorous wife, Heather.

"There's still a crowd of our lot in the cafe". Heather said pointing across the coach park to the green and yellow fronted building. "Where did you all get to ?" She asked. "We caught the bus to Positano, but it wasn't really worth while, too windy. We did get a nice pizza and a salad for lunch. Of course...Joe and John had chips with theirs". Mavis replied.

"So you really think it was you someone intended to stab, not your sister". Joe repeated. "For goodness sake Joe, we've stopped talking about that. You'll get Jenny upset again". Mavis scolded. "It's alright Mavis, but I know who the someone is". Jenny squawked in anguish.

"You and Joe and John and Lucy, oh and Edith and her sister have been such lovely friends, there's not been many on the coach that seemed to like me and Jenny for some reason. Sorry we left you for the second half of the tour but we just couldn't stand another minute with that woman". Jill said apologetically

"Envy and jealousy my loves, that's the problem with this bunch of characters. As long as you had a good time and you don't regret your week with the Swiss boys, that's all that matters". Lucy gushed joining in the conversation.

"We really did have a great time. I hope they keep their promise and we do meet them again". Jill sighed and immediately began to weep. "I think those lads have had a big affect on you, am I right ?" Lucy probed. "Yes, I'm in love with Isaac and I know Jenny is with Axel. We have each others addresses and numbers and we have told each other we will definitely be together again, but I'm afraid once they get back home they might forget all about us". Jill said sorrowfully.

"I watched how those two lads treated you and Jenny at the wedding and at the reception, they won't let you down, I can tell". Mavis interrupted to settle Jill down. "How lovely, a holiday romance, I could do with one of those". Lucy quipped.

"Do they live somewhere nice ?" Mavis enquired. "Yes, it's beautiful, it's a hotel, but it's a typical Swiss chalet. It's only a smallish hotel but they have a farm as well. They live there with their parents and a younger brother and two older sisters. The oldest sister was the one who got married. They all work running the hotel and the farm. But they are very wealthy. Apparently their grandfather built up a chain of hotels throughout Switzerland and Austria which their dad inherited. Their parents bought that red Mercedes for Axel's eighteenth birthday, the car you saw when we went up the Eiger. And Isaac had a Jaguar sports car, but his is only a two door. That's why we used the Merc". Jill gulped excitedly before pausing to breath again. "My dad bought me a book for my eighteenth". Jenny chipped in.

"You did well there then girls. Mind you they wouldn't have stood any chance if I was twenty again". Joe quipped with a cheeky grin. "He's always been a big flirt, even when we were courting, he just can't help himself. Mind you he was a handsome sod, still is but he's harmless". Mavis responded. "Ignore him girls, hell go away". She added as Jill gave him a playful smack across the back of his head.

"Who are we waiting for now ?" Someone from the rear of the coach called out. "Just waiting for the red lump, I think". The familiar voice of Dug the bug replied. "Let's go then driver, give her a basin of her own medicine".

"Why the hell have we put up with her for the whole holiday ? Surely one of us should have had the guts to have reported her. Did you and Jill know her before at all ?" Tom voiced, an elderly widower travelling alone, one of the two solo guests, both very short in stature, no taller than five feet each. The other his new found holiday companion, also named Thomas and also a widower but some twenty years his junior, both very likeable and friendly men known affectionately on the coach as the 'diddy men'.

"Somebody already has phoned the office and complained, David and Ffion the Welsh couple did. Ffion told me last week, but she was frightened in case RD found out because they think she has been sacked, that's why she's finishing at Naples once we've gone".

Edith whispered leaning into the aisle suspended by her seat belt.

"She probably blames you two girls, she thinks it's you that's reported her. That's why she's had it in for you". Another of the obnoxious gang suggested. "She's had it in for us two since we first stepped from the plane in Salzburg". Jenny snapped.

"I think we are all entitled to a big refund. Why don't we all sign one complaint letter before we get to the airport. Douglas, you're the one with the notepad, draft something out". Joe requested.

Having sat quietly reading his newspaper for the past half an hour the driver swivelled in his seat and stood facing down the bus with his eyes searching for any empty seats. "Is it just Rose we're waiting for, is any one else missing ?" He asked. "I can only afford to give her another twenty minutes or none of you will catch your flight". Giovanni retorted. "Sod her let's go, give her a taste of her own medicine". Douglas shouted bravely, repeating a previous comment, then looking panicky towards the coach door.

"She wasn't in the cafe". Came the softly spoken voice of a timid elderly lady seated by the window, with her belt already fastened next to her husband's empty chair. The quiet elderly couple had gone practically unnoticed throughout the holiday mainly due to constantly being sat amongst the obnoxious set,

"My husband isn't back yet". She cried nervously. "No Jack's not here". A friendly companion relayed her words to the driver.

"Is this him". The driver asked as a tall sturdy, robust looking gentleman climbed ungainly from the taxi that had drawn alongside of the coach. The harassed man in his early seventies clambered on to the coach. On his way down the aisle to his seat he profusely apologised to the coach as a whole, and explained that he hadn't realised how much time he needed to visit Amalfi.

"Oh that, I went a flyer, I tripped over a loose paving in Amalfi". He responded to someone who asked him what he'd done to cause the large patch of dried blood on the back of his right hand.

Meanwhile Jill and Jenny sat silently watching the rivers of rain water racing down the windows, whilst directly opposite, the wife of the creepiest of RD's followers, a pathetic couple of fiftyish year olds, nudged her husband. Philip her husband then past a derogatory remark to his wife about the tear in Jenny's skirt, just loud enough for the teenager to hear. "Just a slight mishap, nothing to get you excited about". Jenny snapped as she draped her coat across her lap to cover her exposed leg.

We're going to have to leave now, will someone get those cats off the bus please". Giovanni screeched, and reopened the automated door to allow Heather to shoo the two stray creatures that had suddenly decided to leave the security of their hiding place beneath a seat.

"I can't afford to wait any longer, one hold up in the traffic and you will not catch your flight". Giovanni advised his passengers.

"Just a moment". He requested as he bent his head forward towards his private radio mounted on the dashboard.

"Well that settles that then, Rose won't be coming back to the coach now I shouldn't think, she's wanted for attempted murder". Giovanni explained and turned up the volume on the radio. "The police are currently searching for a yellow and red coach". He added.

The constant buzzing noise of chatter immediately fell silent for several minutes before gasps of horror echoed around the coach. "I said all along that she'd stabbed Jenny's sister". Joe shouted angrily.

"Let me try and get you all to Naples airport before the police catch up with the coach". Giovanni called out but even before he could start the engine a Polizia car drew to a screeching halt in front of the coach and a second car pulled alongside. The two uniformed officers from second vehicle impatiently banged on the coach door as it began to open. Giovanni explained that RD hadn't returned to the bus. After a quick search through the bus and a long discussion in Italian, with the passengers all anxiously looking on. The officer instructed the driver to opened the hold and removed RD's personal luggage. With time all important one of the police officers demanded the tour itinerary and a full list of passengers and contact numbers which Giovanni produced from RD's folder.

"The police want to know if any of you have any idea where she went". Giovanni asked. "She was down in Positano in the restaurant when we were there a couple of hours ago. Jill and Jenny saw her last waiting at the bus stop". John from Gateshead uttered.

Jill and Jenny looked nervously at each other but were relieved and glad that they weren't even questioned following John's information.

After Giovanni had relayed the relevant information, the senior of the officers signalled with a wave of his arms.

"We're free to go now folks, fasten your seat belts. We going to have a police escort to Napoli". Giovanni called out using the microphone and then tossing it into a pocket on the central console,

By the time Giovanni had started the engine, the leading polizia vehicle was already in position blocking any traffic to allow the coach to access the busy roadway.

The coach moved speedily away with a small number of passengers looking intently for any sign of RD. "I don't know why anyone's looking for the murdering bitch, she's not likely to be coming back to catch the coach". Joe shouted.

"It's a pity we didn't know they were after her, we could have got her caught there and then in the restaurant". John retorted.

"My God the atmosphere without that

woman might feel a bit eerie but it's a damn site better". Joe announced as he half turned to the rear to speak to Jill and Jenny.

"What are you up to now, leave the girls alone, they're probably as fed up of your daft comments as I am". Mavis said while dragging him back sharply by his left arm. "I was only going to say......". "Well don't". Mavis snarled. "About the trial when they catch her". Joe continued to complete his sentence. "Thank God you didn't". Mavis replied angrily.

With many of the party now asleep in an array of poses and others straining to stay awake, the coach travelled at great speed following the polizia escort vehicle to the airport.

Jenny sat staring vacantly at the patterned plaid back cloth of the seat before her. Her eyes glazed over with tears, though not actually crying but making an occasional sniffle. With both hands securely holding the cardboard box containing her precious Murano figurines laid on her lap, and with Jill at her side to comfort her, and the thought that Rose Devlin was supposedly a fugitive and with her sister out of danger, Jenny allowed herself to relax for the journey home. "I'm just going to phone Isaac". Jill informed her. "Axel will probably be driving". "Ask him to ring me the first chance he gets". Jenny sighed, and then strained to try to listen in on Jill's conversation.

"We don't need to worry about her any more, it's over now, RD's not going to be coming back, the police probably think she's hiding somewhere waiting to get on a flight". Jill muttered quietly. "She's got what she deserves. Thank God Diane is going to be alright". Jill added just as quietly.

"What now !". Exclaimed Tynesider John, seated with Lucy at the front of the bus as the driver careful eased off his speed and slowed to a halt as instructed by the flashing sign displayed at the rear of the escort car.

In an instant all four police officers, two from each vehicle where standing menacingly waiting for Giovanni to activate the door.

As soon as the door opened, two officers charged beyond the driver and positioned themselves, one remained near the front and the other hovered around half way along the aisle leaning on the top edge of Jenny's seat.

The third, and apparently the most senior officer held a conversation in Italian with the coach driver for several minutes which ended in what sounded like a bit of heated frustration by Giovanni.

With the officer now returned to the leading escort car, the passengers turned into a rowdy rabble demanding an explanation for the new hold up.

Giovanni raised the microphone to within a few inches of his mouth. "I'm very sorry folks, but I've now been instructed to follow the police escort vehicle to their head quarters in Napoli. I'm sorry but you won't be catching your flight after all. I tried to argue with the officer but he refused to give way".

A few of the party became hostile and threatened violence towards the two police officers. These were some of the obnoxious group and fortunately to their benefit the officers did not appear to understand the English language.

The noise inside the coach increased in volume with everyone confused and frustrated demanding to know why the coach is not now going to the airport. "I don't know either". The driver half turned and angrily shouted down the bus in retaliation to someone suggesting he must know the reason.

"For God's sake, someone tell us what's going on, most of us have got people waiting the other end, we've got to fly home today". Another angry voice screeched from the rear end of the bus, echoed by several other irate passengers.

For once Joe became the voice of reason and stood in the aisle. "If Giovanni says he doesn't know, he bloody well doesn't know. We should know him well enough by now, he's been on our side since day one. We might as well just wait now till we get to this police head quarters and we'll find out. And all we can do is hope they'll be quick and let us get away. We're a bit ahead at the moment with the escort, we might still do it. So leave the driver alone and let him concentrate on driving the soddin' bus". Joe said ending in a mild rage.

Jill and Jenny looked nervously at each

other as the coach moved slowly through the busy streets of Naples following the escort vehicle, eventually entering an enclosed parking area protected by a robust chain link fence, The leading car peeled off to one side to allow Giovanni to site the bus immediately opposite the rear entrance to the Polizia station.

"Everyone stay exactly where you are for the moment, and be very careful what you say". The officer currently leaning on Jenny's chair called to the far end of the bus as he snapped in retaliation to an indignant verbal insult from an angry guest.

"Well he can speak English, my God he's been called some different types of animal in the last hour". John whispered to Giovanni. Giovanni smiled as if he knew all along.

Soon the whole coach was again in chaos, impatient for an explanation when the most senior of the officers climbed back onto the bus. "We need to catch that bloody plane !" The cry went out, repeated and shouted by many of the passengers as if it were a football chant.

The police officer spoke quietly to the driver before they both left the coach and entered the building. "Surely it's not Giovanni they're after, wonder what he's been up to ?" Dug the bug squeaked. "Well it can only be something to do with Rose, so why couldn't they have waited till he'd got us to the airport ?" Another hostile voice bellowed.

"Well we're definitely not going to make

the airport now whatever happens". Joe called out above the din. "I wonder if there's a later flight tonight". The younger of the two Toms asked hopefully. "No idea but even if there is we won't have a driver if they hang on to Giovanni and it'll most probably already be fully booked". Joe answered.

"What about you two lasses, you must have your parents or someone at Gatwick waiting for you". Joe enquired. "No...we'll just get the National to Bath, no one will miss us, we share a flat together near our hospital". Jill responded leaning across Jenny from her window seat position.

Over half an hour of uncertainty and unrest passed by, overseen by the two onboard officers before Giovanni returned and casually sat back in his seat, resting his arms across the wheel.

"Thank goodness now perhaps we can get going". A rarely heard Scottish accent was detected above the noise, just as a plain clothed, tall, skinny, sun tanned middle aged man with greasy long black hair, slicked back into a short pony tail, neatly clipped with an elastic band entered the bus and immediately picked up the microphone.

Firstly he issued what sounded like an order or a warning to the driver in Italian and then after a couple of taps on the head of the microphone, turned his attention on to the passengers.

"Everyone.......please collect all your coats and belongings from inside the bus and make your way from the bus and go through the door opposite......no talking to the driver". He demanded and beckoned the first of the guests to move forward.

As each person entered into the long corridor behind the door they were ushered along and seated on one of the not so comfortable upright row of chrome plated steel framed chairs with blue plastic seats.

As soon as the coach was free of all it's passengers and checked for any left behind personal items, two uniformed police officers assisted Giovanni to remove everyone's luggage from the hold and stacked it against the outer wall, protected from the weather only by an overhanging open sided canopy.

Most of the guests were getting a bit uptight and panicky and second guessing what they were going to do next, when the four people seated at the top end, or head of the queue were herded individually through four separate oak coloured wooden doors numbered one to four. Once inside the small rooms, each person was questioned by an officer accompanied by a second officer to witnesses their statements.

All those seated stared as the first door reopened after about twenty minutes and watched as the occupant was directed through a door at the far end of the corridor, there to be held in a large rear conference room until every passenger has been interrogated..

As one room became empty the next person seated at the head of the queue was ordered to go to the room number displayed on the door, in a manner reminiscent to a doctor's surgery.

Jill and Jenny fidgeted and whispered nervously to each other as their turn drew nearer. Another door opened and their friend Joe emerged and was routinely escorted in silence passed Jill and Jenny without even glancing in their direction.

Edith held on tightly to Georgina's hand when her time to be called arrived and after consultation between several police officers the two sisters were allowed a joint interview.

Jill visibly began to shake when a finger indicated her turn and feared even more as Jenny immediately received the call.

After almost three hours the last of the passengers was escorted from the corridor to rejoin the rest of the party and without any further delay, all except the two girls, were lead back out into the yard and on to a waiting bus.

The driver stood holding a microphone urgently wanting to make an announcement, prevented by the din of everyone talking loudly and shouting hysterically, all at the same time.

"Why the hell have they kept Jill and Jenny, what have they done, why were we all asked questions about them. Why did we have to sign statements ?" Heather asked while fighting back her need to be sick.

"They knew who they wanted so why didn't the police just take the brats off the coach and let the rest of us get home". An obnoxious lout of a man dressed in only a string vest and grubby jeans, bawled from one of the back seats, generally reserved by him and his wife and their travelling friends.

Although this particular gruesome foursome were hated and avoided by the rest of the guests, several other passengers voiced their agreement with the man's sentiment.

A fight was begging to begin as John the ex marine and Brummie Joe simultaneously fled down the aisle and stood menacingly over string vest man and his just as disgusting mate, with fists at the ready, although giving away at least ten stone in weight and about sixty years in age between them,

Common sense eventually prevailed as several other passengers intervened, with Joe and John secretly happy to have escaped unscathed and with their dignity intact.

"You've no idea what the girls have supposed to have done". Joe spouted off again in response to another set of verbal insults aimed at them. "I'd say they've caught the wicked bitch and to try to put some of the blame on Jenny and Jill, she's accused them again of stealing her money, the bugger". Joe suggested.

"Or they've done her in. That girl Jenny threatened to kill her enough times, and they didn't know she was wanted by the police until we were back on the coach. That's why we were all asked questions about them and had to sign statements. And they were the last to see her, Geordie John told us that". Creepy

Philip screeched with his voice raising another octave with every additional word.

"Will you all please be quiet". The driver bawled with the aid of his microphone for the fourth time. "For goodness sake....quiet !" He added as mayhem threatened to erupt again.

"Is everyone here ?" He asked after the passengers had finished shuffling around the bus and eventually settled almost in silence into their seats, leaving one empty double seat half way along the forty seater coach.

"Right then, it's getting late now so let's not waste any more time. I'm going to drop you off at a hotel quite close to the airport. You're booked on an early flight in the morning, so I need you all outside by five fifteen". He added, but before he could continue with his instructions a voice called out above the dull chattering. "Where's our luggage ?"

"Don't worry, it's safe, it was all transferred to this bus while you where in the cop shop, but you can only take your hand luggage into the hotel. There just wouldn't be enough time to mess about repacking the coach in the morning". The driver insisted.

The same voice interrupted for a second time. "Let's hope the hold is cleaner than the inside of the coach".

"It's an old bus and it's cleaned every night. I can only apologise if you're not happy but this vehicle has been running around all day ferrying workers to building sites and factories. That's what it does, so it gets in a bit of a mess by this time of the day. It'll be spotless when I pick you up in the morning. Your luxury touring bus is off on the reverse tour tomorrow morning and had to go into the workshops for a service and a valet". The driver added and after having a sip of coffee from a flask carried on with more information.

"And by the way, a bit more bad news, Heathrow, Gatwick and Luton are closed due to a terrorist threat, so all flights are being diverted. I understand your flight is now scheduled to land at Newcastle".

"That'll do me pal". John from Gateshead called out. "The flight you should have caught today has been diverted there. Mind you half an hour earlier you could have been on it. It was delayed by about three hours due to the uncertainty of the situation. It's probably just about to take off any minute now. Anyway let's get moving and get you to the hotel". He concluded and skilfully manoeuvred the coach between several stationary polizia vehicles and into the evening traffic. All at once the coach was alive with shouting and chatter.

"The police knew who they were after so why didn't they take the girls off the coach in the first place and let the rest of us get on that flight". Philip said repeating his earlier outburst. "If you've got nothing new to say keep your gob shut, you creep". Joe warned, turning to eye ball him.

The heated conversations for and against the girls, mostly the latter, continued throughout the ten minute ride to the hotel.

"My God, is this it ?". The elder of the

Toms exclaimed as the coach halted outside a three storey building looking in dire need of restoration.

The noise level remained high as the coach emptied and everyone piled into the confined hotel lobby. Surprisingly well appointed and a complete contrast to it's external shabby appearance.

"By the way, who's paying for all this ?" John enquired when it got to his turn at the desk. "Don't worry sir, it's all been organised, I'm sorry to hear some of the comments about the state of the building, but I think you'll find the rooms to be more than satisfactory and our facilities to be first class. Here's your key sir, room two one four, it's on the second floor". The smartly suited male receptionist responded.

Another gentleman, also looking very elegant in a dark grey suit and plain pale blue tie, announced himself by name and then confirmed that he was the hotel manager. Standing with his back to the door he advised the party that there was a late meal now ready in the dining room and that a packed breakfast would be available for collection from the reception desk in the morning.

~~~~~~~~~~~~~~~~~~

Day seventeen Tuesday

"My daughter phoned me last night, she drove down to Gatwick to pick me up but she said they weren't allowed to get anywhere near the airport. I told her our problem and that we were going to be landing at Newcastle, so she set off back home. She was going to drive all through the night to be at Newcastle to meet me. I hope she's been alright driving all those hours on her own". John said to the listening group as they stood in the chilly early morning air.

With the guests all grouped outside the hotel, shuffling around on the pavement to keep warm, noisily discussing and still arguing over the previous day's events, the yellow , bus displaying it's red demon logo along each side and across the front and rear, drew carefully in to the kerb.

"Good morning ladies". The driver greeted in a sombre tone of voice as he helped a couple of elderly ladies on to the bus. "Thank you driver, you speak very good English". Georgina the eldest of the sisters eagerly complimented. "That's because I am English my lovely. Born and bred in Nottingham". "Did you know this Rose Devlin woman that all the mystery was about yesterday ?" Her sister Edith asked as the pair sat in the front seat on the opposite side of the driver.

"No I don't get involved with the touring

and holiday side of the company. I only work part time transporting workers morning and late afternoon and on to about seven". The driver replied, withdrawing to his seat as the rest of the passengers boarded the bus interrupting his conversation with the sisters.

"It's only a fifteen minute drive to the airport. "Have any of you seen the news this morning ? Well I can tell you folks that you are all very lucky people. Your delayed flight that you should have been on has apparently disappeared over the North Sea. According to the Italian news report, the last contact air traffic control had was over northern Germany".

Gasps of horror and a few shrieks from the ladies interrupted his reporting.

"They're not sure whether it's an accident or linked with terrorism. There's been no siting of it landing or crashing on land, so at the moment they are assuming it must have come down in the North Sea". At this point several of the women on the coach began to sob with sorrow, and possibly relief that they had the good fortune to have missed the flight.

"Poor old Jill and Jenny, they're in an Italian nick, but if it wasn't for them we'd all be dead. So you owe your lives to those girls !" Joe shouted loud enough for all to take note.

"Driver, would it be much trouble for you to take me and my sister to the railway station ? we've decided we don't want to fly". Edith asked hopefully. "Of course, but are you sure you can manage on your own with your sister. I know she's not well, my mother is a sufferer just the same. It'll cost you a lot and it'll take a few days. You'll be in the UK in three hours on the plane, are you really sure ?"

"Yes my sister is very frightened and I know she won't get on the plane, we've just been discussing it". Edith replied. "Okay then if that's what you want stay on the bus". The driver answered and pulled into the airport coach terminal.

The airport was extremely eerily quiet and an air of gloom was apparent as the party en-mass wheeled their luggage in to the main building, nervously contemplating their flight home.

The news flashing around the terminus screens supported the assumed claim that flight number B84389YX had crashed somewhere in the North Sea with the loss of 96 passengers and eight crew members.

The Italian police were visible a short distance from Positano searching an area where they suspected that Rose Devlin went missing. Two officers watched from the road while a colleague abseiled the cliff face looking for any indicative markings or clues. Below and being tossed perilously close to the rocks, a couple of divers searched for any sign of a body from a rigid inflatable dinghy.

In the meantime Jill and Jenny were still being held in custody in separate cells at the Napoli Polizia head quarters, only to discover

to their horror later that day that they would
be both held on suspicion of the murder of
the holiday courier and transferred to be
detained in separate Italian prisons

~~~~~~~~~~~~~~~~~~~

Soon after they had been contacted by their daughters the girls parents accepted the advice from their respective solicitors and elected to employ the services of a highly reputable law firm as recommended.

Over the following weeks the appointed lawyers failed to obtain bail for the girls but continually debated with their Italian counterparts and eventually secured the girl's release on the grounds of a lack of sufficient evidence, but soon after Jill and Jenny had returned home and thought all their troubles were in the past, they were stunned by a phone call from their lawyers.

The Italian prosecution service decided that their main item of evidence, a brief hurried mobile message sent by the victim to her tour company head office in Bristol, supposedly sent moments after she was allegedly attacked by the girls is after all a genuine call, and they demanded that the British police rearrest them and charge them with the murder of Rose Devlin.

"I'm very sorry but the Italians are insisting that we do not allow bail and asking for extradition, so I'm afraid you're going to spend your Christmas's in custody. But at least you are back on British soil which is to our advantage. And I think we can convince them and the Home Office to let the trial take place here. That's about all the hope I can give you at the moment". The lawyer informed as she sat facing the two weeping teenagers while being overlooked by a female prison warder.

"Oh Jenny, I nearly forgot, you asked about your twin sister, she's back in America now and apparently going to make a full recovery, and your present has arrived at your father's house and it's all intact, and according to your dad it's got pride of place in his display cabinet. And here's a letter the Italian authorities redirected to our offices, it's been opened by them, it's from your dad. He obviously sent it not knowing you were back in England". She concluded.

"Oh no !" Jenny exclaimed, scanning quickly through the correspondence. "Dad thinks the Murano figurines are his birthday present. He thanks me for his card and the wonderful present. All I said in the card was his present was to follow. Oh well at least It'll be safe with him. He thinks the likeness of the figure's faces is uncanny and he loves the inscription on the glass base. Good old dad". Jenny said affectionately.

"Patience is the name of the game for now I'm afraid. I'm not allowed to discuss the case at this meeting, that will be done with each of you individually immediately after Christmas, but rest assured we will scrutinise every scrap of evidence". The lady lawyer said emphatically.

The two girls were then lead away to be transported back to their separate prisons some seventy miles apart.

Almost a month passed by before the Italian justice system reluctantly released the relevant evidence, having held off in an attempt to force the extradition of the girls back to Italy to stand trial.

The most incriminating items of evidence was Jenny's diary and the mobile telephone message, purporting to be that of a desperate plea from someone stricken at the base of the cliffs with serious injuries and in danger of being swept off the rocks into the sea.

All the statements given at the Italian police head quarters by the driver and all the passengers were of a similar nature. The majority confirming the consistent bullying and ill treatment to the point of hatred of the girls by RD. But all told the same incriminating information that Jenny had repeatedly threatened to kill her. The remainder contained more or less the same text but far more hostile In their wording, actually accusing the teenagers of revenge for the alleged assault on Jenny's sister.

Otherwise the only other pieces of evidence to note was firstly, Jill's rain hat was found a few feet below the cliff, caught up in a clump of brambles. The other being a small gold locket on a tiny broken chain containing a picture, said to be, by RD, her boyfriend, which was found hooked on top of the stone safety wall. Both items accompanied by a photograph substantiating the location of the alleged assault.

The most telling piece of evidence being the lack of a body. And with the Italian legal system conceding to the trial taking place in the United Kingdom, a date of some four months ahead was set for the combined trial of Jenny and Jill, with both the British and the Italian Prosecution Services agreeing that a conviction for the joint murder was the only outcome.

"It's a bit ironic that your arrest in Italy saved the lives of the rest of your party, but that's not much comfort to you in your predicament". The appointed barrister said before he introduced himself and explained the criminal court procedure.

"Your QC will be representing the both of you in court, he's a brilliant lawyer so keep your chin up. Before we look at the evidence against you, first.....tell me, did you or your friend do what the prosecution is charging you with. Did both of you or either one of you, accidentally or deliberately, push Rose Devlin over that cliff to her death". "Definitely not, we left her at the bus stop and never saw her again". Jill replied emphatically, although visibly tense and nervous.

"Right then, just try to relax. My name is Peter...Peter Worthington. I'm a barrister and I'll be assisting your QC in court....We'll just go through the evidence step by step to prepare your best defence". Jill looked on terrified as he produced a grey folder and removed a batch of various coloured documents.

"I think that's about it for now, I think we've covered everything for the moment. One thing in our favour, and the reason the Italians initially released you was their lack of a body. With no body and no woman named Rose Devlin, apparently this was a false identity and there's no record of her to be found". Peter the barrister retorted confidently.

"Why did she use a false name ? Do you know who she really was ? How do you know this ?" Jill asked with a bit more optimism in her voice.

"We have an old associate, he's an ex Chief Police Inspector now living in Southern Italy, he has a villa about thirty miles from Amalfi. He worked with our law firm for a number of years before he retired to Italy. He's assisting us". Peter replied cautiously and without any further explanation continued with more information.

"All their evidence rests on the call this Rose Devlin made to the Red Demon Continental Holiday Tours company office in Bristol, we've now got a copy. It's very sketchy but the wind and the noise of the sea does make it sound authentic. The most damaging aspect of the call other than trying to state her condition is that you can clearly hear her words. 'them girls'. Apparently the Red Demon office confirm that the receptionist put the phone to voice mail for an hour while she had her lunch break. That's why there was quite a long delay before the police commandeered your coach. But I don't suppose you had any reason to realised this".

"Does Jenny know all this ?" Jill asked and immediately began to cry. "Not yet, you're the closest so I came here first. I've an appointment to see her on Monday". Peter replied.

"Tell her I'm fine". Jill shouted as the woman prison warder escorted the barrister from the room.

~~~~~~~~~~~~~~~~~

THE TRIAL

"All rise". Ordered the court usher as Judge Sir Henry Leadbeater entered the court room.

Jill and Jenny stood apart either side of the court room, each accompanied by a female prison guard officer. They glanced nervously across the room at each other, forcing a half smile as the judge delivered the charge against them.

"Jennifer Rodgers and Jill Peters, you are jointly charged with the murder of a woman known to you as Rose Devlin by physically pushing her over a cliff near the town of Positano in Italy in September last. . How do you plead. Guilty or not guilty ?"
"Not guilty". Two timid voices answered.

The usual court procedures followed with the accepting and swearing in of the twelve jury members, seven men and five women, with the most senior looking lady elected to be their 'foreman'. The CPS and the defence lawyers then outlined their respective cases.

With all the formalities completed Jill and Jenny nervously scanned the foreboding court room and looked anxiously towards the public gallery at their parents. Jenny had to take a second look to convince herself that it was her mother seated next to her dad.

The prosecution lawyer called their first of the half a dozen of the coach holiday passengers, before Judge Sir Henry called a halt to the proceedings to rebuke the CPS lawyer for the repetitiveness and informed the court that he would rely on the written statements and that there was no reason for any more of the tour bus party to be called. "Next witness".

"That's a bugger". Peter whispered to James Hargreaves the defending QC. "They've called the English lady from the bus stop. I let her go because I considered her to be hostile". "We'll see". Replied the QC calmly. "How were they traced ?" He asked. "Our ex police chief in Italy located them". Peter replied. "It's a pity he couldn't locate the taxi driver who took this bloody woman Rose away". Hargreaves snapped annoyingly.

The prosecution completed their questioning of Mrs Howe exacting only the information they requested, that she saw Rose Devlin leave the bus stop and follow shortly after the girls, and that she did not see Miss Peters hat get blown from her head.

"Was there any conversation between the defendants and Miss Devlin during the short time they stood at the bus stop ?" James Hargreaves asked Mrs Howe politely.

"The girls chatted to me and my husband for a few minutes before they decided to start walking". She answered.

"And did Miss Devlin speak after the defendants had left ?" James asked.

"Not to us.....we left her on the other side of the road and sheltered from the wind for a few minutes in an alleyway before we went down into Positano....but we did hear her shout after the girls....I think it was 'I remember you two, I'll get you' ".

"Thank you Missis Howe. I've no more questions for this witness". The defence lawyer said quietly glancing to gauge the jury's reaction as he returned to his chair.

The whole court then listened in a hushed silence to the recording of RD's mobile telephone call to the tour operator's Bristol office.

Sighs of nervous disappointment could be heard from the public gallery when the words "them girls" were clearly spoken.

"I think we'll leave the jury to come to their own conclusion regarding this important piece of evidence". The prosecution announced with a degree of satisfaction.

"I agree with my learned friend". QC James Hargreaves concurred sharply.

After a further half an hour devoted to a report on the sea and the weather conditions on the day, the court adjourned for the end of the first day.

****

The morning newspapers were having a field day with headline stories depicting the case as the alleged murder of a non existent woman who was herself wanted for attempted murder of the twin sister of one of the court room defendants.

Rose Devlin being a false identity she

concocted to gain employment as a courier with the Red Demon Holiday Company as the intended courier fell ill at the last possible moment, leaving the company with no other option at such short notice than to take this woman on trust with her false name and references as a last resort.

****

Over the next couple of days the defence QC batted away the revelations of the events recorded in Jenny's diary and the finding of the rain hat on the cliff side and also the gold chain and locket, containing a miniature photograph of James Dean, or his double. The rain hat and the locket supposedly identifying the location of the alleged assault.

He also emphasised the important significance of the attempted murder of Jenny's twin sister as being strong motive for Rose Devlin to suddenly disappear just as an arrest was imminent, which the prosecution insist is irrelevant to this trial.

The prosecution lawyers again persisted to the judge's irritation to allow all the coach passengers to be called to the witness box.

Judge Sir Henry repeated his denial and showed his annoyance towards the prosecution lawyer by dismissing all those who had managed to attend, instructing the jury to rely on their written statements.

With no further relevant witnesses Judge Sir Henry Leadbeater called on the prosecution to address the jury.

"Members of the jury. The fact that a body has not been found does not mean that there isn't a body......Miss Devlin was a strong robust woman so it would have taken the combined effort of both the defendants to have physically pushed her over the stone safety wall down the cliff face to her death.

You must dismiss any sympathy for a revenge motive, we do not accept an eye for an eye in the British legal system. Rather than a reason for Miss Devlin to abscond, the fact that the defendants strongly suspect that she had attempted to murder her twin sister in Venice on the assumption she mistakenly thought she was murdering Miss Rodgers was in fact the strongest possible motive for revenge, and that they did in fact murder Miss Devlin.

Perhaps you consider there's a possibility that Miss Devlin fell accidentally in the ensuing struggle between the three women, if so you must return a verdict of not guilty of murder. But I believe with all the evidence the court has heard you will decide she fell as a result. of an attack by the defendants with the deliberate intention to kill her.

Then there's the numerous statements from the coach passengers and the driver, all thirty nine of them, confirming that Miss Rodgers repeatedly threatened to kill or harm

Miss Devlin. And also confirmed by both defendants themselves from their original statements and again from the witness box.

Then of course we have the mobile phone call Miss Devlin made to her company office, you've all listened intently to the content of that call. You've heard that she lay injured on a ledge at the base of the cliffs with the horrendous waves breaking over her which eventually took her life, and that she new she wouldn't survive so she was determined her killers would not escape justice. This was the action of a woman knowing she was going to die.

Then there is the rain hat, Miss Peters stated that it became dislodged the moment they left the bus stop, but Mister and Missis Howe were still at the roadside and they said that they never saw it happen. And then the locket caught up on the ragged stone wall. The only logical solution is that the fragile chain was snapped in the fight and unknowing to the defendants it became lodged on the wall". The CPS lawyer continued for a further quarter of an hour revisiting every minute drop of incriminating evidence

After a seemingly endless but convincing speech, the prosecution lawyer concluded as expected with the established narrative, requesting they return a unanimous verdict of guilty for the joint charge of murder".

****

"They're not confident in winning this so they're now hinting at a new trial on a manslaughter charge". James Hargreaves whispered to his barrister assistant and stared vacantly towards the public gallery before rising to his feet and strolling calmly over to face the twelve jurors, carefully avoiding eye contact with any individual member. He began his summing up in a quiet but clearly audible pleasant manner.

"Ladies and gentlemen of the jury. The fact that a body has not been found is because there isn't a body". He emphasised his opening sentence. "Rose Devlin or whoever she is, is a spiteful, bitter, jealous woman who bullied and tormented the defendants to the point of malicious hatred. For what reason we will probably never know. Forcing these two nineteen year old girls to leave the holiday they'd dreamed of and paid for.
I ask you know to consider that this woman who was hated so much by most of the passengers as well as the defendants did not die at the hands of these two unfortunate girls on trial before you. But is still alive and most probably residing and working back in Switzerland using yet another false identity. The whole thing being a vicious set up by her to implicate Miss Peters and Miss Rodgers and at the same time eliminate any further interest in her involvement in the attempted murder of Miss Rodgers's identical twin sister.
The fact that Miss Devlin attempted to

murder the defendant's identical twin sister, mistakenly thinking it was the defendant herself could be a reason for revenge. But in this case I ask you to consider that it is also the strongest possible of motives to implicate the defendants, whom she openly displayed an overwhelming hatred, in a very clever plot to fake her own death in order to disappear. After all there never was a Rose Devlin.

The plastic rain hat....Miss Peters said it was blown from her head and flew over the cliff where it eventually landed, and that she chased after it for a few seconds. Miss Devlin watched and appeared to ridicule Miss Peters's chase. So it blew from her head, in those conditions completely reasonable. Once the two girls were out of site Miss Devlin followed and located the rain hat and there and then decided to stage her own death at this location. She then planted her locket on the stone wall, firstly snapping the fragile chain.

She then recorded the sound of the gale force wind and the noise of the sea crashing against the cliffs some seventy feet below. At the same time pleading convincingly in a scratchy voice for help and saying that she had been pushed from the cliff top with her final two words, 'them girls'. If you listened very carefully the latter words were quite distinct compared to her plea for help. Therefore I ask you all to consider that this message that was received, but not acted on for a further one hour was an elaborate hoax call. In fact it was a pre-recorded message.

You will also have heard the evidence why Miss Rodgers and Miss Peters decided to leave the coach and that Miss Rodgers suffered injury to her upper arm from being deliberately pushed to the platform at the summit of Jungfrau mountain railway which the prosecution dismissed as an accident.

Then there was the malicious accusation of Miss Rodgers at the hotel in Lucerne when Miss Devlin openly lied about having her wallet containing a considerable amount of money stolen. For some inexplicable reason the matter was not mentioned again, although you've heard from one witness that he constantly reminded her.

And let's not forget the words by Miss Devlin as witnessed by Mister and Missis Howe. 'I remember you two, I'll get you'. What did she mean to do ?

I ask you to consider the nature of the character of these three women and make up your minds as to who to believe.

And finally the matter of Miss Rodgers's torn skirt. She stated that this occurred in contact with a sharp corner of rail when she alighted the bus on the journey back to Sorrento, and you will all have seen the statement from the bus company.

I could bore you for another hour but I know that you are all intelligent people and have listened to all the evidence. If you have the slightest doubt in your minds whether the defendants committed the crime of which they are charged then you must return a verdict of not guilty". QC James Hargreaves concluded.

****

For several minutes Judge Sir Henry Leadbeater advised and cautioned the jurors before they retired to consider their verdict.

With no sign of an imminent return of the jury the court was adjourned until the following morning.

Jill and Jenny stared across the courtroom at each with fear in their eyes as they were led away separately from the court.

****

The chatter of expectation became silent as the twelve members of the jury filed back into court. Jill and Jenny looked terrified and both were visibly shaking as they watched the proceedings and the confidence being displayed by the prosecuting lawyers, smiling and whispering.

Jill's anxiety and near panic proved too much and fearing she was about to feint, sat on her seat, only to be forcibly lifted back to a standing position as the judge entered the court. With both girls now standing with tears tracing across their cheeks, trembling and terrified, The judge asked the jury lady foreman. "Have you reached a verdict upon which you all agree ?" "Yes your honour".

The court room suddenly started buzzing as a court usher burst into the room and requested to approach the bench.

The unsettled judge then ordered the jury foreman not to disclose the verdict for the moment, and that all the members of the jury remain silent.

"We'll take a short recess". He ordered and immediately left the room instructing both sets of councils to accompany him.

The packed courtroom was in a state of confusion as the noise level increased in anticipation of a major announcement. The newspaper hacks were fervently tapping away on their mobile phones searching for any scrap of information. For the first time in four months the girls sneaked an opportunity to speak to each other from their isolated positions. Jill mouthed across the room. "What's going on ?" Jenny stared back bewildered, but before she could reply her lady prison warder intervened.

The noise abated in an instant when Judge Sir Henry Leadbeater and the QC's re-entered the court room. From his lofty perch the judge banged down his gavel to silence a couple of talkative newsmen who had excitedly just received the latest relevant news report.

The court waited in absolute silence with all eyes focused intently on the judge as he repositioned his microphone to speak.

Firstly he stared at Jill and then at Jenny. Both the girls averted their tearful eyes as he gave them a compassionate smile and spoke in a soft voice. "You're both free to go... ...release the prisoners".

Both the girls looked stunned and sunk down into their chairs and burst into joyous uncontrollable sobbing.

The judge then turned to the jury foreman and all the jurors and ordered each of them not to disclose or discuss their verdict either deliberately or accidentally for fear of prosecution.

The information was still limited to a few newsmen but it rapidly spread throughout the court room, although not many appreciated the significance that a small yellow water tight bag and been recovered from the North Sea by the crew of an oil rig safety boat. The majority of the packed public gallery including the girls parents could only look on in bewilderment.

The yellow bag which had been found a few days earlier, but only when it had been received by the airline investigators was it found to contain a lady's passport and a mobile telephone.

The passport was immediately scanned and emailed to the court office. The mobile phone still in good working order revealed the most astounding information, the last call being made to a Sorrento based taxi firm and the penultimate message made by Rose Devlin to the office of the Red Demon Holiday Company.

After the court had been cleared, the

girls now totally exhausted and confused and reunited with their respective parents, all in tears with a mixture of joy and relief. Jenny looked at her mum and dad as they affectionately held hands, and smiled realising that they were now reunited.

"If you'll all follow me". QC James Hargreaves requested as he lead the way to his chambers. "Right, now you young ladies, are you feeling a bit happier?" James joked as he summoned his secretary to fetch some refreshments. "Yes, but what has happened?" Jill asked. "Have a comfortable seat and I'll explain". He said to the girls standing hugging each other.

"Do you recognise the woman in this passport photo that we've just received?" He asked both girls as he turned the screen in their direction. "It's RD". Both girls screeched in unison. "Janis Harris". Jill murmured as she studied the name accompanying the passport photograph. "We knew a Janis Harris from school, but my God if it's the same person she's changed". Jenny exclaimed. What's the address on the passport?" Jill asked at the same time reading it for herself on the screen.

"Oh my God it is her, we lived two doors from that address and Jenny lived on the opposite side of the road. We were still in the juniors when she left school. The last time we heard of her she was in a young offenders detention centre. Jenny had been the only witness against her when she stabbed a lad in our school with a flick knife. She was always a vicious bully, in fact the whole family terrorised the street". Jill retorted in amazement at finding the true identity of the Red Demon.

"I can't believe it, she must have seen our names on her passenger list and then recognised us at Salzburg airport and decided to get Jenny from the minute she saw us. To think she went as far as to almost kill Jenny's sister by mistake and then to try to get us put in prison for her own murder". Jill added, fuming with anger.

"And just for your interest I can tell you that the Italian police found the flick knife with which she attempted to murder Diane in her holdall they took from the coach in Sorrento". Peter Hargreaves announced.

"We did consider using this in court had it been necessary". He added. "I wonder if it was the same knife she almost killed Jimmy Armstrong with". Jenny remarked.

"And now we'll never know whether we did or not". Jenny chirped, transforming the atmosphere with laughter as she got to her feet and cuddled up between her mum and dad.

"We're not going to know either". Peter Worthington and James Hargreaves echoed.

"And by the way.......one more surprise. There are two handsome Swiss lads waiting patiently outside in the corridor".

The End.

Thank you for reading my story I hope you found it interesting and enjoyable.
I would be very pleased to receive your comments
You can review this book on Amazon books.

Yours sincerely   t.a.wood

current book titles by t.a.wood

"Mary"
"Missis Hooper"
"Two Yellow Dresses"

Available on Amazon Books

Printed in Great Britain
by Amazon